Crack the Spine

Summer 2013

Edited by Kerri Farrell Foley

ISBN-10: 0988978237
ISBN-13: 978-0-9889782-3-2

Library of Congress Control Number 2013947545

Published by Crack the Spine Press, LLC.
Printed in the United States of America.

Crack the Spine Press, LLC
Houston, Texas
Hattiesburg, Mississippi
www.crackthespinepress.com

CONTENTS

To Serve and Protect

It was one of Becky's last softball games of the season. Marne pulled her Taurus wagon into Hilldale Park's parking lot that breezy July evening and before even getting out of the car and gathering the cooler, the blanket, the bug spray, she checked in the rearview mirror to make sure her smile was on straight and that there were not too many visible smudges on the plate glass. Walking over the soft, damp, freshly-cut field to the diamond where she saw bodies wearing the red and blue Meteor team colors, Marne breathed in the green smell of newly-cut grass and felt relieved that her heartbeat sounded rather slow and steady for a change. All she wanted that evening was to sit, relatively undisturbed, adoring Becky's nimble grace. She wanted to cheer, like the other parents, when and if it was appropriate, and she wanted to end the day lying on her side of the queen bed with a heart beating softly enough to let her sleep.

With these small goals in mind, Marne spread her blanket on a one-person-sized spot on the top row of the bleachers. She was just a few minutes early, but already knew which parents would likely soon show up and where they preferred to sit. Tiffany's mom, Judy, was the next to arrive. She nodded politely to Marne and sat a bleacher below her and to the right, where she made a show of inspecting her nails, rings, watch. Marne knew she was saving places for Samantha's mom, Ellen, and Amy's mom, Diane. She also knew that all three would chatter the evening away with precious little notice of Marne.

Marne had always felt like she was on the outside looking in. And although she knew that a lot of people probably felt that way, she still couldn't shake the belief that those other people probably only periodically felt that way, like when they lost a nice-paying job or struck out with the cutie in line at the Superamerica or maybe when they got a little behind on their credit card payments. But she was pretty sure they didn't *always* feel like an outsider, not like she did, because she'd seen them normally and happily interacting with each other by the thousands, so knew that they felt accepted and appreciated by at least some other human beings at least some of time. Marne knew this because she was a great observer of people, being stuck, as she was, behind a giant sheet of plate glass. Behind the glass, she *was* separate from everybody else, *couldn't* really connect with anyone, even when it might look like she was, and so, she understood that she had little choice but to try to be content enough in watching the goings-on of others – the happily adjusted, to be sure – but even those others who Marne suspected occasionally felt lonely or isolated.

"I brought popcorn," Diane shouted to Judy (certainly not to Marne) in her screechy smoker's voice as she climbed up the bleachers. Diane must have just had a pedicure. She had strange-looking rubbery things between her toes. They stuck out of the top of her sandals.

"Oh, goodie," Judy yelled back.

Marne didn't say anything, even though she liked popcorn. She knew she wouldn't be offered any.

Marne first became aware of the sheet of plate glass surrounding her when she was in kindergarten. Mrs. Schultz always started the day in what she called "circle time." Looking back, Marne realized that Mrs. Schultz, besides likely needing an inordinate amount of structure and control, was probably trying to foster a sense of community among the twenty-five freshly-sprung five-year-olds in her charge. Marne had seen the same attempts at forced camaraderie throughout her whole forty-six years of life; Brownie Girl Scout circles turned into church school circles which turned into biology lab groups which turned into dorm governing committees which turned into regular employee meetings at the weekly community newspaper where she worked designing and laying out advertisements. Every leader beat the same idea of a circle to death more times than if that circle theme had been a long-stored community of dusty rugs. The splendor, the beauty of each individual would eventually emerge with enough forced community. Melded striation must eventually produce brilliant multifaceted tapestries. Each thread would retain its own individual purity while contributing to the panoramic big picture. Standing that first day of kindergarten, not yet in Mrs. Schultz's circle, Marne already knew she was a thread of no easily-defined color. She'd even decided that she quite possibly had no color at all, which is probably what made it so difficult for others to fix her for long in their gazes, to address her, sometimes even to notice her.

Judy patted the bleacher space next to her. "Let's get this party started."

Diane laughed her smoker's laugh and sat next to Judy. Diane was careful not to bump Marne's legs. Marne discretely slid her blanket a few inches to the left so they'd all be more comfortable.

"Ellen's not coming," Diane said.

Judy frowned and made a whimpering sound.

"Migraine," Diane said.

"Poor thing."

"Poor thing nothing. Too much red wine."

"I've heard that, too. Red wine and migraines," Judy said.

"You can never be sure."

"That and certain cheeses," Judy said.

"That and certain husbands," Diane said.

"Oh, go on."

"Frank could make me hit the red wine."

"You love Frank."

Mrs. Schultz had said, "Come into the circle, children, and hold hands with your neighbors." Quickly all of the other children obeyed and stood clasping each others' fingers and palms while Marne, still rooted on the slate gray linoleum near the door, noticed that her heart was suddenly beating especially loud. "Come, dear," Mrs. Schultz said to Marne. But Marne couldn't move. She could feel her feet sticking to the dirt or glue or gum that must be on the tile beneath her, could hear her own heart pounding so distressingly. Mrs. Schultz temporarily left the warm glow of the circle and came to kneel in front of Marne on the linoleum and to peer at Marne through the plate glass that Marne was suddenly first beginning to see. Mrs. Schultz asked Marne why she wasn't cooperating, why she had chosen not to listen to her brand-new teacher on the first day of school. Mrs. Schultz wondered, she said, if Marne realized that she must obey her teacher, just like she obeyed her parents, and also wondered if maybe Marne was feeling shy.

Marne knew, of course, that obedience was expected in school, and had no problem with that. She also knew that she wasn't feeling particularly shy, for she understood that to be the feeling she had when her Mommy wanted her to play *Chopsticks* on the piano for the mailman. The problem, Marne tried to explain, was that she lived at the end of a dead-end street, a rural gravel road that, especially when Daddy would come home in his big truck every Tuesday night, Mommy would call the road to nowhere. And the one thing Marne knew she didn't have on that gravel road was neighbors. Mommy talked about that all the time, too, how life would be so much easier, happier, better if they only had some neighbors. "I don't have any neighbors," Marne consequently explained to Mrs. Schultz over the embarrassing sound of her beating heart.

Mrs. Schultz had smiled, then, had crinkled the corners of her eyes into a web of wrinkles. "Why sure you do, sweetheart," she'd said to Marne. "Everyone in the class is your neighbor." Marne, stuck as she was on the linoleum, peered around the kneeling Mrs. Schultz at the circle of smug, smiling children all clasping the hand of someone else, both left and right, and she didn't recognize anyone. Not only that, she knew, like a horse knows it's going to rain, that with her alarmingly loud heart and all, she simply didn't have it in her to pull her feet up off the linoleum in front of everyone and pry anyone's hand from anyone else's. Those hands, every one of them, were locked together in sweat and grime and baby lotion, and they would not give way for the likes of a stuck-footed, loud-hearted neighborless Marne.

A heavy-set man lumbered up the bleachers. He sat next to Marne and held out his hand. "Name's Frank," he said. "Sam's dad."

Samantha was the Meteor with the bad knee who hung longingly against the chain link fence in front of the Meteor bench.

Marne shook his hand. "Marne."

"That's Becky's mom," Diane said.

Frank rolled his eyes in mock amazement. "Oh, Becky."

"Now, Frank," Judy said, "What would Ellen say?"

All three hoo-hawed about something Marne didn't understand.

And so Marne had stood on the slate gray linoleum, alone, behind her sheet of plate glass on that first day of kindergarten. She wasn't trying to be difficult. She just couldn't react any other way. Mrs. Schultz must have thought it best to leave her to her own devices, stuck as she was, helplessly beyond any reasonable reach, with her five-year-old heart beating, beating, beating, because Mrs. Schultz joined the circle she'd effected and proceeded to lead the other children in a variety of get-to-know-you games and songs. Marne thought most of the other children looked like they were having fun, certainly looked comfortable enough. And after what seemed like hours, but what was likely only fifteen minutes, Marne felt her feet unsticking and noticed that the plate glass surrounding her was evaporating and that her heart was again beating quietly. She would join the circle tomorrow, she decided. And just when she'd reached her decision, Mrs. Schultz sat them all down for story time and Marne instinctively sat down almost exactly where she had been standing, on the slate gray linoleum near the door, which on second thought, was really much too far from the little piece of carpet at the other end of the room.

And so it was that whenever Marne felt ready to move from her patch of gray, her feet or legs or arms would rebel and would move almost on their own, in a different direction, without her, which ended up keeping her in the same narrow place. It was a horrible way to start kindergarten. Looking back, Marne could certainly understand that much. And even though Mrs. Schultz patiently and persistently coaxed Marne to join the other children, and it truthfully was only a matter of days before she did just that, Marne could never shake that feeling of being on the outside, behind the sheet of plate glass with her feet stuck to the linoleum, looking in. That feeling of separateness, of being on the outside of the circle, never ever left her.

"Say, mind if I share your blanket?" Frank asked Marne. "These bleachers are hard on the hiney."

Marne minded very much, but stood almost before Frank had finished speaking and started to unfold her blanket. "Of course," she said. "I don't know why I didn't offer earlier. You without a blanket or cushion or anything."

"Thanks. We can just fold it like this so there's plenty of cush for each of us."

"Plenty."

Diane raised her eyebrows at Judy. Judy stuck her hand into the bag of popcorn.

Marne had always felt separate, even when she was one of the go-to members of the junior debate club, or when she went to the prom her senior year with a respectable-looking Italian gymnast, or even when she graduated with distinction from Lakehart University. True, she had learned to clasp hands, to sing along, to mimic the facial expressions of the included. But underneath everything, if she listened closely, her heart still beat distressingly loud and her feet had a tendency to stick and her vision was often clouded by smudges on the glass around her. She even felt separate when she sat on the top row of the bleachers, sharing a blanket with someone.

All of this gave her a potent level of self-reliance, which, Marne guessed, was the silver lining of her cloudy world. She had learned to be content with herself, most of the time, and to accept her separateness as a fact of life, albeit a sometimes lonely one. Once in a while, Marne wondered how other people would react, if they knew the truth about her and her stuck feet, beating heart, and real honest-to-goodness plate glass. They'd likely wonder how she came to hold a fairly decent job designing and laying out advertisements at the community newspaper. They'd also wonder how she had come to marry Gary, who was now a partner at Brook, Grasslyn and Steel. They'd definitely wonder how she had come to guide and nurture her amazing daughter Becky, who at twelve, was a flute-playing, straight-A student as well as hot-shot short-stop for the club fast-pitch softball team. Oh, yes, they'd wonder all right. They probably already did.

"Hey, Frank. Want some popcorn?"

"You ladies know how to take care of a guy."

Frank dug both hands into the bag and spread a pile of popcorn on his lap. He cupped handfuls and stuffed the kernels into his chewing mouth, like he was feeding an assembly line.

Marne rummaged around in her cooler, found her bottle of water and large ziplock bag of red seedless grapes. Fruit was better for you than butter and salt encrusted carbohydrates. Marne occasionally allowed herself a handful of popcorn if Gary bought a tub when they went as a family to the latest Disney movie. Movie theatre popcorn was better than the stuff you make in the microwave bags.

"Hey, you gonna share?" Frank asked Marne, eyeing her grapes.

"Oh, certainly," Marne said holding the open bag out to him.

Frank helped himself to a good-sized sprig. "Wow," he said. "Where'd you get these?"

"Gronahan's. They have the best –"

"Produce!" Judy and Diane said at the same time.

"Hey," Frank said, pointing the sprig of grapes at Diane's feet. "What's that growing between your toes?"

Marne guessed other people wondered about her because she wondered about them. She wondered how they so breezily floated through minutes, days, entire weeks without hearing their own pulses, and she was sure they wondered how she survived at all. Marne survived because she had to. She looked at her life to this point as being a series of ever-harrowing bridges she had forced herself to walk over. The first bridge, the one she gingerly stepped onto after graduating college was one of those rustic wooden bridges you sometimes see in old parks. It's a little worn, has a plank or two missing, but is rock-steady and sure. Marne crossed that bridge when she landed her job at the newspaper and started designing and laying out the weekly advertisements. Her job let her practice human interaction. Not because she worked with a plethora of people or had meetings or conference calls or anything remotely close to what made Gary tick like Big Ben. But because she had to read all the ad copy and had to place the pictures and artwork so that everyone else could be guided along socially-acceptable routes. Marne was the first to understand that whiter teeth and fresher breath made people like you, that large-framed sunglasses were making a comeback, and that you should get a mammogram each year, every year, after 40. Marne secretly blessed whatever serendipitous force cleared the way for her to have this job. It was her school, her muse, her crutch. Understanding advertising gave Marne a leg-up on understanding people, and that's exactly what ultimately enabled her to have white enough teeth, fresh enough breath and the right shaped sunglasses to make an adequate impression on Gary when he was still a junior partner doing mostly second-tiered research for the other lawyers. She studied, he reacted, and when the time was right, Marne knew the best places to shop for engagement rings and bath towels.

Marrying Gary was the second bridge Marne forced herself to cross, a little wooded thing with high sides, shaking and swaying over a churning river. This bridge had several missing slats, but those little holes were nothing that a young, spry woman couldn't discern and hop over, even one whose personal plate glass sometimes thickened and made images look a little lumpy, a little distorted. As Marne baby-stepped down the aisle, she understood that she also gladly walked across that wobbly, swaying wooden bridge and met Gary – normal Gary – on the other side of it. She told him "I do," of course, yet could say, and can still say with a fair amount of candor, that she didn't love Gary, had never really loved him in that trembling, juicy way the modern world defined love, which wasn't so unusual for her. When had she ever reacted like she was supposed to? She simply admired Gary and his well-managed law career. She liked how little he forced her to speak and was happy that, being a little far-sighted, Gary didn't notice when Marne was feeling especially lonely or isolated, which would have been embarrassing beyond belief and something neither of them were probably capable of facing, let alone fixing.

Thirteen years later, Marne still sometimes forgot she was even married, still sometimes held her breath when Gary would come home from the office, first wondering with alarm who was coming through the back door, then, upon remembering Gary's step, becoming bizarrely afraid that somehow he'd finally come to, and would begin to really know and understand her. Maybe he would be able to hear her freaky beating heart or would notice that she was enclosed in ever-thickening vision-distorting plate glass. But Gary, buried as he usually was behind tomes of legal briefs and newspapers, never noticed either the glass or Marne's heart, which was a blessed relief, especially considering Becky.

"Doesn't Ellen ever get pedicures?" Diane asked.

"Beats me," Frank said. "There are some things a man would rather not know."

"How *is* Ellen?" Judy asked

"Damned headaches all the time."

"I got my first migraine after doing 'shrooms in college," Diane said. "If I'd have only known."

"'Shrooms don't cause them," Judy said. "It's hereditary. That was just a coincidence."

"You say something about an illegal substance, ma'am?" Frank asked through a mouthful of Marne's Gronahan's grapes.

"Statute of limitations, officer," Diane said.

"I sure as hell hope so."

"Game's starting," Judy said.

Judy, Diane, Frank and Marne all clapped and yelled, "Go Meteors!"

Marne watched Becky take her position as short stop. Becky cocked her head and waved to her mother. She was the only Meteor who waved.

Marne considered Becky her biggest challenge, her most treacherous bridge to date. Having her, actually giving birth to her, was nothing compared to the daily interactions being mother to a whip-smart daughter demanded. Marne's third bridge, her Becky bridge, was the bridge she still wasn't completely over. In Marne's mind, the Becky bridge was a rotten rope number flipping and bucking in high winds over a 200-foot canyon deepening with still-bubbling molten lava. She did not want to cross. She did not want to hang there. She did not want to fall. Sometimes, the only *want* Marne was aware of was that she wanted to start over, wanted to maybe take a different, plodding, sure route to the same destination of Becky's adulthood. But, of course, there was no way to do that now, no way to unwind the ambition and gregariousness and curiosity of high-spirited Becky. There was no way to make Becky like some other twelve-year-olds, content watching television, easily placated with excess sugar or fast food. From the beginning, well-meaning Marne had suggested only the best, the most high-minded activities and thoughts and words to Becky, true to the ad copy she not only put together but critiqued, and Becky, brilliant child that she was, had glommed onto each worthy suggestion without regret.

"Tiffany's pitching?" Diane asked.

"To start," Judy said.

Diane stood and yelled to the center fielder, "Amy, you're too far back!"

Marne noticed that Becky was in perfect position. She always was.

"Hey, who's serving cocktails later?" Frank asked.

Marne had survived twelve years so far, as mother to Becky. She frequently slapped a friendly smile on her face and turned up at all the requisite meetings and programs and recitals to support her daughter, to give her a chance at the inner circle. That Becky thrived was no surprise to Marne, though Marne was aware, of course, that other parents were occasionally surprised about Becky's confidence and good-natured success. "That's your daughter?" they'd ask, changing the emphasis from "your" to "daughter," depending on which connection they'd found most unbelievable. And it was during conversations like this that, although Marne smiled woodenly and even managed to nod her head, she also clutched even more tightly to her rotting rope bridge, terrified it, or she, wouldn't hold, or hold on, for the long haul after all.

It was the top of the third and the score was 4-2, Meteors. The A's were batting. Tiffany wound up and threw a sizzler. The batter hit a grounder and started running. Becky stood perfectly positioned, crouched, with her hands in front of her. The ball was bouncing along the infield and Becky watched, calculating how she should position her glove. After the second hop, the ball landed in her glove like it was magnetized. Becky pivoted and threw in one graceful motion.

"Out!" the first-base ump called, pumping his right fist over his head and behind.

"Thata girl, Becky!" Frank yelled. "She's a natural," he said to Marne.

Marne smiled. She knew Becky was good, very good.

"Amy, move up!" Diane yelled.

"Let the coach coach," Frank said. "You've got to respect authority, Mom."

Diane smiled and sat back down. She dug around in her tote and produced a pack of Newport Lights.

"Oh, you're not going to start already," Frank said. "Usually you need a few first."

Diane smiled at him as she tapped a cigarette from the pack, held the pack to her lips, pulled a cigarette out with her mouth and lit it with a red disposable lighter.

"Jesus," Frank said.

"Free country, Frank," Diane said on an exhale.

"I've got margarita mix in the freezer," Judy said.

"Sold," Diane said. "But Frank can't give me a ticket when I drive home. Your margies are lethal."

"I'll watch your back," Frank said. "Serve and protect."

"Judy serves and you protect," Diane said.

Judy, Diane and Frank laughed.

It was the bottom of the fifth, two outs, bases loaded. Becky was up to bat. The pitcher had walked the three Meteors on base. Marne thought the pitcher seemed nervous. She kept darting her eyes to her coach who was giving her a constant barrage of signals. Even though Marne was rooting for Becky to get a hit, her heart went out to the nervous-looking pitcher who was throwing way too many balls. She understood how awful that pitcher must feel, how alone, how isolated. Marne's own heart started pumping sympathetically.

The pitcher threw three balls, which Becky patiently resisted swinging at.

"Take it, Becky!" Frank yelled. Then he said to Marne, "You probably don't know what that means. Do you?"

"Take it!" Judy and Diane yelled.

Marne froze. Her heart started beating a little louder. She'd been uncovered. She'd been to countless softball games, true, but there were still a few (well, maybe more than a few) of the finer points she didn't understand. And, of course, she had never asked anyone anything.

"Come on. What does 'take it' mean?" Frank asked, stuffing popcorn into his moving mouth.

"She should take a swing?" Marne asked.

Frank chuckled. Judy and Diane exchanged glances. Marne knew she'd made a grave error.

"No. Take it means take the walk. Resist swinging. Like she's doing," Frank said. "Becky knows."

"Take it, Becky," Diane yelled again.

The pitcher wound up and delivered a fast ball, one of Becky's favorites. She could hit any fast ball. Anyone's. She didn't resist. She couldn't. She swung.

"No!" Frank yelled. "It's a pop up!"

Becky ran like the wind, but the center fielder was in perfect position for the catch.

"Yer out!" the ump yelled. "That's three."

"Big mistake," Frank said.

"Becky can't resist a fastball," Diane said.

"That's the trouble with kids these days. They can't resist anything anymore. She needs to put the team ahead of herself."

"Now, Frank," Judy said, glancing at Marne. "Her mom's right there."

"Sorry," Frank said. "Hey, got any more of those grapes?"

Marne handed him the rest of the bag. Her heart was beating a little louder now, a little faster. She felt sorry for Becky, who was walking with her head down to the bench. The rest of the team was flying past her, racing for their outfield positions. None of her teammates gave her their usual high-fives. Marne felt Becky's disappointment. It wasn't fair. Becky usually did exactly what she was supposed to. This was one little mistake.

"Sometimes people can't help it," Marne said. She noticed the plate glass thickening a little between her and Frank.

"Sorry?" Frank said.

But Marne couldn't speak again. Her throat was dry. She drank some water from her water bottle.

Top of the sixth. The Meteors were warming up. The first base person threw one to Becky. It was fast and beyond her reach. Becky lunged, but missed it, then glanced in the direction of her mother. Marne cringed behind her plate glass. Ka-boom, ka-boom, ka-boom went her heart.

"Say, what happened with that kid?" Diane asked. "That wasn't you, was it, Frank?"

Frank coughed out his mouthful of popcorn, then sputtered, "Hell no."

"What kid?" Judy asked.

Marne was afraid they meant Becky. Marne stared straight ahead at the Meteors, who were in position, ready for the first A's batter. Marne took deep breaths. She wondered if Frank or Judy or Diane could hear her heart.

"The kid who was accidentally suffocated as they were taking him in. Right, Frank?" Diane said.

"Terrible mistake," Frank said. "The guy involved feels awful. We're not allowed to I.D. the cop, so don't ask."

"But you know him?"

"Sure. Great guy. Wouldn't hurt a fly. Hopefully, the papers will drop this shit. Ruin a good man's career. Everyone makes mistakes."

Tiffany wound up and delivered a lobbing ball. The A's batter slammed it, but caught it just underneath. Becky eyed the fly ball, was rocking back and forth on her heels, waiting for it. Something, a gust of wind, or maybe the spin of the hit, made the ball suddenly drop. Becky was too far back on her heels to get to the ball in time. It dropped right in front of her outstretched glove.

"Wake up out there!" Frank yelled. "Jesus, Becky's falling apart."

"Let the coach coach," Diane said with a smile.

Marne blinked rapidly.

"They're saying he was suffocated?" Judy asked. "The kid."

"From what I hear, he was pretty troubled," Diane said.

"Sure was," Frank said. "Only 18 and everyone on the squad knew his name."

"But it was mostly minor stuff," Diane said. "Right?"

"Listen. Nothing's minor at 18," Frank said. "Kid like that skipping school, selling pot, stealing stop signs. It's only going to get worse."

Tiffany was still pitching, was still looking strong. She was throwing no balls, just strike after strike. The A's were swinging.

Becky was flustered. For the first time in her young life, Marne thought, her daughter's feet were sticking. Marne understood what Becky must be feeling. Her panic, embarrassment and separateness.

"Shake it off, Becky," Marne yelled. She was surprised to find herself on her feet.

"Hey, she's fine," Frank said and pulled at Marne's shorts to get her to sit down again. "Let the coach handle her."

A bulky A's girl strutted to the plate, eying Tiffany. Marne thought she could hear Becky's heart. Or maybe her own was just beating loud enough for two.

Tiffany threw a rocket and the batter hit a line drive. It sailed by Tiffany's outstretched glove and headed straight towards Becky's ribcage. Becky positioned her glove, stood slightly to the side. The ball landed with a whump, smack in the middle of Becky's glove, then popped out again.

"She's bobbling!" Frank cried.

"Get it, Becky," Diane called as Becky stumbled over her stuck feet and tried to pick up the ball bouncing around her.

"Safe!" the ump yelled as the batter pounded over the base.

Marne's heart was pumping even faster now. Even louder. Her vision was getting cloudy. The plate glass was getting thicker. But Marne was relieved she could still see Becky. Becky's image was a little blurry, sure, but Marne knew just which red and blue blob was her daughter.

"They say his parents just got divorced," Judy said.

"Just? Like two years ago," Frank said. "No excuse. The law's the law."

It was the bottom of the sixth. The A's were ahead now, 7-4. The Meteors were fighting back though, swinging and hitting and tearing around the bases. A new A's pitcher was in. Marne thought she looked confident. She wasn't letting the Meteor's attack get to her. She pitched strong and steady.

"I heard the parents are going to sue," Diane said.

"Of course. This is America, isn't it?" Frank said.

"Disgusting," Diane said.

"They probably need the money," Judy said. "With the divorce and all."

Amy was up. The pitcher was still throwing strikes, but they were losing some of their bite. Amy took a strike, then hit a double, hitting in two runs. Diane, Judy, Frank and Marne cheered. It was now 7-6, A's, with two outs.

The bases loaded again. Becky was up. She walked to the plate and got into her stance. Marne thought she looked hesitant. She wasn't crouching enough, seemed to be pulling her neck back.

The pitcher took a breath and blew it out. Was she finally getting tired? Her coach was signaling like mad. She nodded, adjusted her cap, wound up and threw the ball low and outside. Becky held steady.

"Good eye," Frank yelled.

The pitcher threw two more balls before the coach walked the ball to her and had a little chat. She nodded fiercely. Becky was still stuck in her half-crouch. Her neck was still pulled back.

"Protect, Becky!" Frank yelled. "Know what that means?" he said to Marne.

Marne didn't really care what it meant. All she cared about was Becky. She wanted to protect her daughter from defeat, disappointment, shame. She wanted Becky's heart to proudly keep a quiet rhythm, to beat confidence through her 12-year-old veins, like it always had. She wanted Becky to have every advantage. She wanted Becky to triumph.

Marne's heart pounded in her ears. Her vision pulsed with the booming, despite her rapid eye blinks. She felt the rope bridge swaying beneath her.

"Protect?" Frank said again. "Capiche?"

"I know what protect means," Marne said, looking him in the eye. "It means to keep safe, to not risk anything."

Diane and Judy smirked. "Protect, Becky, protect!" They yelled.

Marne's eyes smarted, probably from looking into Frank's. She blinked back some wetness.

"Hey, hey," Frank said. "It's okay. I didn't mean anything."

But Marne could no longer see him. The rope bridge's swinging had picked up and the plate glass had suddenly grown so thick she could barely see color. She focused her eyes on the half-crouched blob that she knew was Becky.

"It means swing away," Frank said. "You could yell that."

"Was it murder, Frank?" Judy asked. "The kid?"

"What? Murder?" Frank said.

"But the paper said –"

"It was self defense. The kid was spitting at an officer. With AIDS and all that, you can't be too careful."

"I thought you can't get AIDS from saliva," Diane said.

"That's what they say this month. An officer has to protect himself and his community. He's the authority. Kids got to learn to respect that," Frank said.

The pitcher glanced at her coach who was standing quietly, his arms crossed over his chest. Becky bounced on her heels, shook her head a little.

"What exactly happened," Judy asked. "With the kid?"

"18 is a man by law. A young man. Responsible for his actions."

"What happened?" Diane asked.

The pitcher stared down each base runner. Then she eyed Becky. Becky bounced again.

Frank was silent for a moment, busy stuffing grapes and popcorn into his mouth. Then he talked while he chewed. "Cop was tailing him, figured he'd be up to no good, Saturday night and all. Pulled him over for suspicion of DUI. Found some weed on him and proceeded to arrest him for possession of an illegal substance."

"How much was on him?"

"Doesn't matter. So the kid resists. He's kicking and swearing at an officer of the law. When he started spitting, the officer called for backup and put the spit mask over the kid's head. Only he made a mistake. It wasn't the spit mask."

"What was it?" Judy asked.

"Gas mask. And the vents weren't open."

"Oh my God," Judy said.

"Innocent mistake!" Frank said and crammed a handful of popcorn into his mouth. "We were never trained."

Marne's heart pounded harder and harder. She felt ill, like she might pass out. Her chest was starting to hurt and the veins in her neck felt like they might explode. "Swing away, Becky," Marne called weakly to the red and blue blob.

"And now the parents are going to sue," Diane said. "Where was their interest in their son when he was alive?"

"Exactly," Frank said. "Troubled kids come from broken homes. They got what they deserved."

"And judging from the path he was going down…" Judy said.

"He was probably better off," Diane said.

Marne turned to look at Frank again. It was suddenly very important that she look at his face. She couldn't see anything but a blurry form from her swinging position behind so much distorted glass. But she could hear him loud and clear.

"He was trouble all right," Frank said.

Marne's heart pounded louder than it ever had before and the plate glass fogged up horribly, probably from the panting breaths she was forcing out. The breeze picked up. It snapped Marne's hair in her face. Marne was frightened, swinging as she was on the perilous Becky bridge. She clenched thick hanks of gnarly rope in her fists. The rope bridge was swinging ferociously and Marne could barely see. Frank's, Judy's and Diane's voices were lost in the wind. With the deafening beat of her heart pulsing through her, Marne clung to the rope bridge, swinging sickening over the rolling lava. She held on as tight as she could and fixed her vision on the strong, bouncy red and blue blur that she knew was Becky. But Marne was getting dizzy from swinging and, suddenly, she lost all balance. She stumbled right, then left. She clutched the air. A great gust of wind slammed her against one side of the bridge. She managed to grab one flopping rope. But then, the bridge itself buckled, tossing Marne into the air, forcing open her bloodied palm. Marne let go. She flew up. She would fall.

Marne floated in the misty air for the longest of seconds above her body, above everyone. And in that millisecond before Marne knew she would be sunk, she saw, with crystal clarity, Becky's strong form swinging the bat and connecting, and she saw the brilliant blue sky and the orangey purple of the setting sun and the stringy layer of clouds that veiled the earth. She saw Judy and Diane throw their arms up, accidentally flinging popcorn everywhere, and she also saw Frank clutching his throat, his face as purple as a plum.

Frank clawed the air, reached feebly around him. Above the bleachers, Marne could see his muddy eyes watering and blinking, like pits in the plum. She could also see Becky fly around first base.

Judy and Diane jumped up and down.

Marne crossed her hands over her pounding heart, then plummeted.

Becky rounded second, then third.

"Yay, Meteors!" Judy and Diane cried.

Just before Marne hit, just before she succumbed to some eternity of velvet blackness or silent fog, something cold and clammy brushed her elbow.

Becky slid into home.

As Marne reveled in the pristine red and blue picture her daughter cast reclined on home plate, her descent halted. She hovered, caught between up and down.

All around her, people cheered, "Yay, Becky! Yay, Meteors!"

For the first time in her life, Marne felt completely calm. She understood everything.

And she was *there*, with a hand, cold and clammy, pawing at her.

Marne turned and stared at the perfectly clear view she had of Frank. His still-purple face. His wildly-darting eyes. Frothy spit had gathered at the corners of his lips. His forehead was crinkled, as if he had an awful headache. She barely hesitated before balling up her fist and making it as tough and brutal as she could. She took a deep, clear breath and swung that fist, hitting Frank hard in his ample stomach. The plate glass exploded outward, throwing thousands of misty shards in every direction. There was a wet pop, as a large Gronahan's grape flew out of Frank's mouth and arched through the air.

Frank lost his balance, leaned backwards too far and, unfortunately, fell off the top bleacher at diamond number two in Hilldale Park. He landed on the ground with a thud.

Nobody heard the thud except Marne. She glanced down to see Frank's pink face and heaving chest, to see his eyes blinking rapidly.

Marne jumped up in wonder, her feet gloriously unstuck, her heart beating quiet as anyone's, her vision clear. "Yay, Becky!" she yelled to her daughter who was being mobbed by her adoring teammates.

"Yay, Meteors!" the rest of the parents shouted.

For Here

For here the bough breaks
and dreams collapse uncushioned
like the smile that forsakes me
and the wonderful illusion of things past
but never lost.
For here I cut my antennae down
and kiss the pyramid on my grass,
blessed by the end result
but never by the happening:
I know the world
and it needs forgiveness.
For here the smell grew toxic
and the glass filled to overflowing
but the grime inside never got better,
though polished every day.
For here I cradle my body to sleep,
the long way down is the only way down
and we are sold by the scars upon our throat,
by the longing discarded that never knew it
could end
and by the only relationship we are all
bound to have – our stronghold with or
not with
God.

Icarus Was the Sun

Esther told herself that God was just taking everyone away one-by-one as an early payment for the rain. That maybe a few more swallowed hearts would appease the empty skies and let the lightning strike with spray. Only then would He let it rain, so that wilted hands and brittle branches would no longer have to claw at the horizon, waiting for the storms, searching for the Lord. Staring stone-eyed at the sun, wondering if He was still there, still listening, still cared about them at all.

The first to go missing was Pooki. Then Daisy, and Sapphire, and a few days later, Duke. Soon after was Amanda Walford, a cute six-year old girl, followed by Donna, Amanda's six-year-old Cocker Spaniel. Rocky was gone in a flash, disappearing shortly after Rex and Joan Crawley. A funeral was held for Amanda Walford the same day that Jackson Everest vanished from his bedroom, along with his Chocolate Lab, Abraham.

No bones ever turned up, no lost dogs were ever seen at the shelter or spread in gore on the shoulder of the road. Search parties were sent out into the desert looking for little Amanda, little Jackson, Mrs. Crawley, and at least 20 others who had seemed to climb into the sky, gone without warning. Here and there were paw prints or dog turds or other ominous signs scattered in the sand amongst the ancient cacti. Sometimes the wind blew so fast and hard that someone would joke that the missing might've blown away. It was the kind of rye humor that was solid enough to laugh at and break the silence of the dunes, but within the thought there was no real cheer. The only kind of humor that seemed to be left in West Riarena.

Life in West Riarena was no longer like a river, with sways and eclipses and swiftness of passage and dull shine. It was no longer predictable or patterned except in the fact that one was either dead or alive. Life in West Riarena was now sharp traffic; dodging collections of nearly-tragic passers-by. One either filled a coffin from death by drought and the starvation and the thirst it so venomously gave; or an empty wooden casket was laid deep enough for the dirt to devour it, but close enough to the open air that it could be removed. For good cause or for worse. For lost-and-found or the increased need for graveyard ground.

Esther had buried her older brother two months ago, Adam filling the coffin that'd been bought years earlier like a baby in a bathtub. His best suit was three sizes too loose, tie looking more like a noose in how it was draped and strung around his thin neck. Her only brother was dead, this brother that had refused meat, even in starvation for his sad suffrage of vegetarianism. When all of the plants died amidst the dust and sunshine, so did such a fragile friend of Mother Nature. Everyone said that maybe God had murdered Mother Nature. Another rye joke in a town too dry for comedians. Esther didn't want to believe it because then that meant that God had murdered Adam.

Esther told herself that God hadn't really killed Mother Nature, that She was only sleeping. And when She'd wake up He'd send the rain, and the flowers would grow and the leaves would green and Adam would wake up and eat corn-on-the-cob like always before. Esther told herself that she wasn't alone.

Parents didn't live as long as usual in West Riarena, before or during the drought. There were too many black widows, rattlesnakes, vipers, poisonous lizards; too much skin cancer, dementia, influenza, malnutrition, fatalistic injury, too many countless ways to die at 50. But Esther had her mutts, all 10 of them, though their numbers had begun to diminish.

Esther liked to give her mutts human names, like Roger and Andrew. There was also Jennifer, Michael, William, Meghan, Kevin, Keith, Robert, and Richard. All mutts in West Riarena were really purebreds, but there was simply no better word at the time for the hounds. It seemed with many of Esther's neighbors that as the drought stole their weight and their health and their families, the mutts were allowed to run free on the streets. Shih-Tzu's and Dalmatians crowded the sidewalks, Dobermans terrorized the few remaining children as they'd try to get to school. But this was not the case with Esther's mutts. They were all she had. So every mutt had their own room in her parent's empty mansion, where they were kept for the night in safety and love.

But around two weeks after little Amanda Walford's funeral, Meghan went missing. While searching for her lost friend, Esther could barely recognize the place she had called home. She felt like she lived in a town with zombies, everyone calling her crazy as she hung up 'Missing Collie' signs on lampposts. They acted as if she was supposed to give up on recovery because the wave of death was so immense.

"My daughter Jackie Lynn's been missing for a month. And you care more about your *mutt*?"

All Esther could do was announce apologies and keep walking, tacking the printed papers onto every phone pole in sight.

The next to vanish was the little Dachshund named William. His disappearance baffled Esther, as he stood only a foot from the ground. Meghan, she figured, could've jumped out the window or somehow opened the door. But William could barely even jump on the couch.

Almost like counting sheep in reverse, by the end of the month only four mutts were left. Phone poles were dressed in black and white pictures of six slobbering faces, Esther's phone number re-stated and re-stated across every page. And now there were no children left to draw boobs or mustaches on her mutts' images, so the papers clung in place through wind and sun, until they'd rip and blow away. They'd litter the sand and cling, punctured, on the cacti. It was as if the desert was a Siren's abysmal arms, pulling away everything in sight.

* * *

Most of the townspeople couldn't sleep out of fear that they'd be stolen away in the night. While parents would cradle their children in their arms through the darkness to protect them from the devouring night, the whole family would go missing instead. But there was never blood, never any sign of murder. Only bed sheets tossed about, belongings knocked flat against the floor. It was this vague means that really painted the town in dread.

But what kept Esther up at night were the eight empty rooms of her mansion. She'd moved Roger and Keith to her room, despite their seemingly newly developed inability to sleep. When there'd been four mutts still left in the house they'd all sit awake by their respective windows, howling at the black sky. In this world, this twisted time, there was only the moon. Cold and gray and alone in the sky. There were no other lights turned on to shine from the heart of Heaven.

As Roger and Keith howled at the new moon Esther lay shivering in bed, clutching her father's pistol tighter. She always slept with a handgun now, one of the few people in West Riarena to even own one. Her house was closer to the desert and further from neighbors than most, once the site of an expansive soy farm. Coyotes had been an issue, but the void had eaten them as well. With the lifeless metal grip sticky in her palm she finally fell into sleep, serenaded by the tearing moans of her only two friends.

Esther didn't awaken until the calls were ripping outside her door. In her delirious half-dream the howls were just the multiplicative echoes of Roger and Keith, bouncing off the high ceilings. As she awoke a little more she figured it was coyotes, no threat, just an annoyance to her and her mutts. But as claws scraped up against the brick under her bedroom windows and slobber sprayed the air with gnarling gums, Esther was anything but asleep. She shot up and readied her weapon, stalking slowly towards the window. As she opened it and peered out she stood in the trap, ignorant of the growling shadow confined to the corner of the room.

In a flash Roger shot out from under the bed and Keith from the corner, each digging their teeth deep into Esther's legs. She didn't so much scream as she did lose half her heart amongst the sound of a tree set on fire. Her pain was not an echoing single shot of resonance into the desert night, but instead a deep sickness like nails grating against chalkboard bones.

Roger was a Yellow Lab, supposedly the picture of family-friendly perfection. But now there was blood on his muzzle, only the reflection of the gray moonlight in his eyes. Keith was much the same, his strong jaw biting down deep enough for both his teeth to touch. But both were careful not to let a drop of blood hit the floor, lapping up all the spills they could as they dragged their master across the room.

Before she was tossed out the window, Esther could see a throng of mutts all roaring below her in the dirt, dragging their vicious paws down her red stone walls. As Keith and Roger dropped her down, Esther glimpsed Meghan, and Andrew, and every other mutt she'd called kin. But head-first against the gray stones at the edges of her garden, Esther fell into darkness, turning indecisively around between thick shrouds of glass shadows.

* * *

When Esther awoke the bleeding had stopped; her scalp burned and hurt, leading her to the assumption that she'd been dragged along by her hair for at least an hour. She was laying on her stomach, sand sticky and dirt thick on her face. The grains felt rough and tasted bitter in her mouth. She longed to roll over, to see the moon and search for God, but her body was too broken. So she lay, panting in the exhaustion of pain, too sick in the freezing, dry air to cry.

"You know what they're doing, don't you?"

Esther screamed and shook at the bite of another voice. There was no energy left in her body to control the polite reactions to anything. She tried her hardest to roll onto her side, to see who was there and whether she could reach the gun tucked into her panties.

"Oh no, sweetheart, I don't want you to see me like this. Not on your last night. Maybe on the way up you'll get to see the moon, at least."

There were too many disasters in three simple sentences to understand at all. Esther just started crying, in an almost relieving way, though this just caused the sand to clump to her cheeks and eyes and freeze in the cold. She didn't have anything to say to another human, so she simply whispered prayers through her tears and assumed they'd reach the sky.

"Don't worry, you'll be on your way up there soon enough."

"Will you stop!"

Finally, some comment came. Shaking and cold and too low on blood to barely breathe, Esther felt her face cake with more sandy tears. Straining once again to turn over and face her supposed last labor in life, Esther fell hard on her chin and bit through her lip, fresh trail of blood tainting the already tear-littered sand.

"The mutts haven't taken me yet because my bones are too thin. They've taken my legs, my left arm; I figure they'll be back for my right soon. Though whether I'll be alive to see it happen is up in the air."

Trying to understand the meaning behind the voice's words was like trying to hear a tambourine through a thunder storm. Every other word would register with Esther and slowly compute. *Mutts. They. Alive.*

Spitting a bloody strand of hair out of her mouth, Esther tried her hardest to speak.

"What about the mutts? Who's doing this to us? What're they doing with your legs?"

The voice shuddered for a second and Esther wondered whether the heart behind it had died. But with the click of teeth and a sniffle it spoke flatly and without pause.

"The mutts are stealing every last soul for miles around this desert. Nile City, West Riarena, Mountville. Just about any place with enough hounds and people who don't dare carry a gun."

"But what for?"

In the urgent eyes of death, Esther had no patience for dawdling manners.

"They're building a stairway of bones, up, up, up, so they can get to Heaven and ask God to give back the rain."

Esther wanted to laugh that rye laugh that folks in West Riarena had grown so desperately fond of. But there was too much sand in her throat, too much blood in her lungs. She simply cried some more, lost under the suffocating weight of the night and death's boot heel on her back. She cried into her lip blood, until finally she passed out again. Though the darkness of unconsciousness was brighter than real life seemed to be.

* * *

"Hello?"

Esther moaned and hissed within her chest, withering with every echo.

"Hello? Where are you? Are you still here? Hello?"

She simply screamed in the silence. The blood of her body had pooled beneath her, ruined the pattern of her lovely black and white polka dot nightie. There was still no moving, right arm asleep under her stomach, left arm twisted and bruised and too tired to move. Her legs looked like a tree after a woodpecker had been at it. Covered in holes and seeping sap into the dirt.

Four legs had a much more recognizable sound than Esther could remember. Then came four more, and four more, and finally too many to keep track. There was no nostalgia to the panting and hot breath at Esther's neck, only savagery and the flavors of a beast she did not know. Finally under the club-like paws of an enormous Saint Bernard Esther was turned over onto her back, dead new moon still trying it's hardest to shine. Breathing the fresh air Esther had about a split second of peace, before once again her forehead shot with pain and an unknown animal dragged her behind them like a toy. Part of her wanted to pass out, but she kept herself awake in fear that if she dived down she'd never swim back up.

For a while the terrain against her broken legs and ripped-up back was the soft of sand, brittle at its worst. But as a collective howling grew in strength and dissonance, a new texture tortured Esther's body. It was not rocks, it was not stone, or pebbles, or hard earth. Squinting across her peripherals as best she could Esther began her shaking again, and bit her lip right back open with shock. Bones. Hundreds of thousands of bones laying chewed and stripped and bleached by the desert sun, one atop another atop another. Skulls, ribs, femurs, and feet. The third layer of filth fashioned itself smugly onto Esther. Aside the dirty sand and the blood there was now the stink flesh of her dead neighbors. But she didn't just take away their grime; for as the mutts pulled her up their mountain, the sharp corners tore open her skin and made a path like baby ruby waterfalls.

Esther's eyes and mind acted like strobe. There was too much terror to see everything straight or clearly. So instead her vision shot in and out, unfocused as her head throbbed with lightening static. But for minutes yet she didn't die, only climbed on her back with fangs in her hair. It carried on for what could've been hours.

There was no making sense of the thin air all around her. One mutt would trade off with another, indicating that this was quite the long trek. And the bones kept piling. Esther couldn't focus on very much, but her mind decided to torture her with visions of the deceased. How many towns now lay empty? How many parents without daughters and sons? She start to cry but exhaustion would scold and she'd slip out but force her way back in. It was World War Three, all within her mind and there would be no survivors to write the history.

Suddenly everything steadied. Esther's head was dropped, and let to fall against a freshly peeled skull. Esther opened her eyes, lashes so thick with blood and tears that they seemed to weigh more than her bloodless body might. She could only feel the cold at this second. The cold of the black sky above, the cold of the gun which still somehow was tucked into her underwear, and most unrealistically, the cold of the moon, directly at level with where Esther and the dogs stood. She gazed with eyes like holes that were trying to steal the moon away from the sun, the gray light her only illumination for the miles of her heart. Without warning her soul felt shock, and unconsciousness came again.

* * *

As had happened in bed, strict barking awoke Esther from her narrow, dreamless din. For a second of eternal optimism she hoped that this was all a dream and she'd wake up to Roger and Keith barking at the morning sun.

The blood in her mouth told the truth.

But when Esther opened her eyes she swore it was to more of a dream than the abyss she'd escaped. Far below she could see the moon, like the beam of a flashlight from so far away. In agony she turned her neck upwards, and felt her stomach pull inside itself. The black space above was rippling in envious blues, glistening as it caught the moonlight. A huge lake, as far as the eye could see, suspended in space. The mutts had finally found the rain.

But they simply barked at the lake, confused by the fact that they were not reflected. Within the depths there were no wagging tails or bloody muzzles. And there was no God above to explain. For each canine face that eyed the rippling plane, only a word dazzled back.

Dog

Dog

Dog

Esther considered this for a moment, feeling like she only had a bean-sized amount of brain left to think with. If every reflection is its original image backwards, was the lake suggesting that the mutts were God? The dogs were Gods? But through it all she wondered where God was. Where was the Lord. Was he hidden in the water, far beyond the surface? Or vanished altogether. Esther's time to ponder this was cut short by her being pulled up to the top of the mountain by her hair, stuck in the center of a circle of dogs all barking at her. Each looking ready to lunge and rip her apart for their case.

From her new view the truth occurred to Esther. Laying underneath the shining pool, she was truly reflected. Her own image, plastered against the boundaries of Heaven. In the absence of God, we are all divine. The soul is as heavy a poem as a thousand scriptures and psalms.

Such bliss was short-lived as one dog stepped forwards, gnashing his teeth and growling wildly at Esther. And at that moment her heart screamed 'not here, not tonight', her veins pumping fire and the blue gleam of the water above. She reached into her panties, pulled out the hand gun, and started firing.

Two dogs fell to the boney ground, another whimpered as a bullet grazed its hind leg and it toppled down the side of the mountain. Esther kept shooting as long as the adrenaline had her, though not enough dogs were falling.

In the smoke and shatter, she managed to catch a glimpse of two dogs coiled around one another, biting at shoulders and throats and bellies. It was Meghan, taking on a Greyhound twice her size. And to the left was Andrew, pinning a Pomeranian with a single paw. All of Esther's own dogs were fighting by her side, against at least a 100 other mutts. A battle in which they had no chance.

Bullet after bullet after bullet, the mass of blood and fur and bones shrunk and threw itself in circles. Esther managed to lean against a stack of skulls and shoot, useless legs tucked haphazardly under her dress. But out of the depths of the fervor came a big white Pyrnees, leaping on top of Esther before the bullet left the barrel. Biting at her firing arm the gun was directed upwards, shot speeding up to the water, striking the depths in silence.

Until there was a rush louder than thunder.

The dogs froze, tails curled and ears peeled back. The thunder grew, and grew, and grew, cracks appearing in the most abstract motion across the calm surface. Until it all collapsed. Miles of water fell down in drizzle and pour on the stairway of bones, the barbarian god dogs, and the one divine light, as she bled beneath the Pyrenees.

Esther's captor didn't cease for long as the rain fell, grabbing her by the leg and dragging her to the rest of the dogs. Hungrily they ripped her polka dot dress, tore her hair from her head. She screamed and cried and punched blindly with her arms and legs in the rain, trying in vain to save herself. The dogs persisted. But the dogs were blind.

The filth of the evening washed away in the rain. The sand dripped down the slopes, the blood wrung clean from Esther's skin and clothes. Her tears were replaced with warm water, hands of calm and softness. The rain all came down quick, and Esther began to rise.

Her ripped polka dot dress was sucked away, her hair lifted from the soiled earth. As the dogs viciously tore her limbs apart and warped her body from the beauty it had been, the pieces floated into the air like dandelion seeds. Jennifer the dog and William the dog watched confusedly as the little bits of cleansed self drifted up, and up, and up, never disappearing, but too far away to tell their height. They shone so bright in their loveliness, white and blue light dust on the remnants of Heaven.

And there was no more rain to pray for, no more God to find. The dogs quit biting at the empty air, some angered by the enviable escape, others distressed by their own sick ways.

A few still howl at the sky at night, staring at the stars that are the skin and soul of a makeshift God. Her enemies will chew their bones, plotting some revenge and breaking the chance for her to end it all safely. They want to pull her down and see themselves reflected, watch her fall and burn at dark. But her friends will dig holes and bury innocent bones, in hopes that someday they can climb back up to Heaven and save her before she comes crashing down. No one can play God for so long; no one could stay so perfect forever.

Esther told herself that stars only shine so lonely for a little while anyway. The rain would come to tear her down, and Heaven would be just gray and dust and night. And everyone would search the skies, asking where She'd gone. Was there anyone up there to listen, or watch, or blame? Everyone's really just alone with themselves, in the end of it all, after all, unenviable.

Emily as Flush to the Light

Never the scamper of the inside,
but the heat, the flesh pressed
against the electric intentions

of an un-tender eye, I have seen
Emily squirm with a splitting
song on censure, I have seen her

tear whole pages into the privacy
of confetti. I think she has started
to feel like maybe the poetry

is hot breath, that I may be a dog
with very few things on my mind.
I am predictably stolen by her.

Paradisu

Aunt Kate started taking art classes in 1950, when Uncle Reg went off to the Korean War. Maggie, her sister and Jen's mother, rolled her eyes. At first Aunt Kate sketched Main Street in the snow. As the snow melted and maple sap made cloudy spots on the sidewalks, she drew more: the county building with budding trees a haze of dots on each side. Then the Minisink Monument, with the Olde Englishe Inne in the distance. Then the library, its crazy pavement and sycamores detailed with smooth watery lines. Her drawings became more precise, her lines more sure, bold yet restrained.

By the time the Episcopal Ladies held their August fair, Aunt Kate had over a hundred sketches and drawings, and even a few watercolors—all of which she contributed for sale. Maggie thought Aunt Kate should have held some of her oeuvre back for her own favorite charity, the Stable Hill Hospital. She didn't understand that Aunt Kate had become impatient with her work and had signed up for an adult education course in oil painting at the high school. By November she was taking the train to New York every week for classes at the Museum of Modern Art. One of the instructors invited her to lunch. She declined politely but asked to see his studio. Eventually, through a process Jen did not understand, Aunt Kate became a student of this man. His name was Luigi Bicciamo, but he called himself Lew Beach.

One Saturday in March Aunt Kate took Jen to New York, ostensibly to shop and see a show. They took the 8:17 a.m. Erie train to Hoboken, then switched to the tube under the Hudson River. Jen held her breath most of the way. She tried to imagine Lew Beach: a romantic figure, tall, long-faced, bearded, with a rich accent.

They got off the train at Christopher Street and went to West 11th Street, where Lew Beach had his studio. Lew was short, pudgy, nearly bald, clean-shaven. His accent was unmistakably New York, with no exotic overtones. He regarded Jen with his black eyes and said "Here's my advice, kid. Keep yer eyes open. The mind will follow."

They walked through the studio. Jen had expected a mass of canvases leaning against dirty walls, a clutter of furniture, easels with unfinished works resting on them, a litter of squeezed paint tubes and ruined brushes scattered about. The studio was, in fact, nearly bare. The tall windows to the north were uncovered, polished clean to admit all the spring light. One canvas was propped on an easel, a few lines sketched on it. In the corner sat a small table and four chairs. On the table were a fresh white cloth, a bowl of apples, a Thermos, and a box of Holland rusk. The floor, except for the area near the easel, was swept clean and dry.

In an adjoining room were Lew Beach's finished canvases. Jen found them alarming. They were quiet, almost peaceful, with a touch of menace.

Aunt Kate talked to Beach about his paintings. Jen listened, surprised. She had imagined a scene in which the great artist was modest and self-deprecating, with Aunt Kate playing the part of the know-nothing secretary, full of awe and innocent praise. Instead, Lew Beach boasted of his great vision, his mastery of color, his intricate brushwork. Aunt Kate responded with sharp criticisms.

"What brushwork? I can hardly make out this thing in the corner. What is it—a Mack truck?"

When Beach proudly showed off a great study of cacti with thrusting arms against a curve of sky, she said, "That looks pretty derivative to me."

Lew roared in response. "Look who's talking! Miss Bushwah from upstate!"

Aunt Kate's icy reply was "Mrs. Bourgeoise," the French word pronounced with precision. To some of her other acid remarks, Beach responded mildly. "Yeah. Maybe you're right."

Lew invited Jen and Aunt Kate to lunch, but Aunt Kate said no, they had shopping to do. In Bergdorf Goodman she let Jen select a gift for herself, not too expensive. The trick was not to look at the price tag. Jen picked out a sterling silver pin in the shape of a horseshoe. It cost nine-fifty.

"Good," Aunt Kate said. She bought the pin for Jen, then took her to B. Altman's, where there was a sale on winter coats. Aunt Kate bought herself a marked-down camel-hair polo coat. Jen bought a pair of Kislav leather gloves. Bearing their packages, they went to Schrafft's for lunch and then to Radio City Music Hall, where they saw the Easter show and *All About Eve.* They came out of the theater into the black rectangular shadows of a late-spring afternoon, then descended into the subway to catch the train back to Hoboken. As they rode the Erie through the darkening villages of Rockland County, they discussed Lew Beach.

"He is teaching me to paint," Aunt Kate said.

"Like him? I mean, will your paintings look like his?"

"I hope not! I like his use of color though. He says that I might just as well say I like his frames—but he is just kidding."

* * *

Jen's friend Bridget had heard a rumor that Lew Beach was Aunt Kate's lover. She couldn't ask anything so blunt, so she asked, "Do you like him?"

"Of course," Aunt Kate said. "Despite his bluff, he's really a very kind man and generous to other artists."

During April Aunt Kate, with Jen's help, cleaned out the former spare room so that she could use it for painting. They had searched all over Goshen for a small office or studio that she could rent, but there was none. There were offices and one-room apartments that might have sufficed, but the owners became uneasy when they learned that Kate wanted it for a studio. Jen's mother finally offered the spare bedroom.

"Just take the curtains down is all I ask," she said.

"It'll be perfect, Mags," Aunt Kate told her sister. "The windows face north; there's a sink in the corner for cleaning up. You won't regret it." She painted every day except Tuesday, when she went to New York to study with Lew Beach. This weekly jaunt was permitted by Sickel, Van Hoesen and Downey, the law firm where Aunt Kate was chief secretary and office manager. On Saturdays she painted all morning. If the afternoon was fine, she went for a drive in her Plymouth coupe, tossing a sketchbook and pencils in the backseat. Sometimes Jen went with her. If the weather was gloomy or damp, they stayed in and read novels or played Casino. On baking Saturdays they helped Maggie in the kitchen. If Jen had to write a term paper or book report, Aunt Kate let her type it on her Underwood.

Jen found it curious that Aunt Kate could be an artist yet have such a mundane life. "It's all in how you look at it," Aunt Kate said. "I put on my old slacks and smock and *Poof!* I'm a painter."

"Is that how Frans Hals started?" Jen asked.

* * *

One day in the following winter, Aunt Kate got a special note from Uncle Reg. He was coming home. It had been discovered that he had a heart murmur and must be discharged from the Navy. Aunt Kate quit her job at Sickle, Van Hoesen and Downey, packed a suitcase, and took a train to New York. She went not to greet Uncle Reg, but to learn more about painting from Lew Beach before (as she told Maggie in a despairing voice) "it's too darn late."

While Aunt Kate was in New York, Jen went down to visit her. Aunt Kate met her at Christopher Street, wearing the polo coat she had bought on their last visit to the city. The weather was warm for March. She wore the coat open over old slacks and a sweater, a bright scarf knotted carelessly around her neck, her auburn hair, uncurled, falling to her shoulders.

"Hi, Suze," she said, using the old nickname they had used for years. Jen felt out of sorts. She wished she did not have to make a weary journey by train under a river in order to visit an aunt who so recently had slept in the next bedroom.

On the way to Lew's apartment, Aunt Kate smoked one Camel after another. They did not go uptown but stayed in the apartment, two blocks away from his studio, where he was still working. His loft was spacious enough to allow Aunt Kate room to work there by herself. Her small canvases, bright landscapes and still lifes, more simple and cheerful than Lew's, leaned against the wall. When Lew came back from his studio, he welcomed Jen with a hug.

"Remember my advice?" he said. "Keep yer eyes open, gal. The mind will follow. *Then* comes happiness."

When Uncle Reg came back from Japan, he brought Aunt Kate six silk kimonos. For Jen's mother, with whom he did not get along, he brought a set of enameled boxes. To Jen he gave a fan painted with images of cranes and ferns. It was a sad time for Jen because Aunt Kate and Uncle Reg were moving to the Southwest. Aunt Kate had sent her belongings back home, as well as all her paintings. She met Uncle Reg at the airport in New York. They ate at the Oyster Bar and saw *South Pacific*. Nothing was said about her month in Greenwich Village.

After Aunt Kate and Uncle Reg had settled in Phoenix, Jen decided to find out more about Lew Beach. She went to the Public Library and Historical Society, but the lady in charge was not a librarian and could not help her. The next day, on a shopping trip to Middletown, she stopped in the Thrall Library and found that they had a current biographical directory of artists on the reference shelf. Here she found an entry for Lew Beach.

"BEACH, Lew, (Luigi Bicciamo), NYC 1908. Educ.: B.A.(Ed.), NYU, 1929. M.A. UChic, 1936. Social worker NYC 1930-31. Studied in Paris (Necker Atelier) 1932–34, 1937–39. Galleries: MoMA, Art Inst. Chic, Bost MFA, Gr. Plains Mus., Galena FA Inst. Exhibits: Paris, 1933; Amsterdam, 1948, Natl Gallery Wash. 1950, 1951, MoMA 1943, 1947."

When photographs of Lew Beach's paintings appeared in *Life*, and when his famous mural *Heartland Dusk* was included in the Museum of Modern Art calendar for 1955, Jen felt a thrill. She knew this man, had been in his studio, in his apartment. "My aunt was his student," she said in the college student lounge, and a caesura of awe halted the conversation.

During her junior year at college, Jen saw Lew Beach for the third and last time. She went to New York with her French class to see *Le Bourgeois Gentilhomme* performed by the Comedie Française. After the matinee, most of the group went to Champs d'Herbes on West 54th Street for dinner. There she saw Lew Beach, looking very much older and leaning on a cane.

"Look!" Jen whispered to Angela, her roommate. "That's Lew Beach!"

"The artist?" Angela said. They hid behind their menus and watched Lew Beach move slowly past them to a table in a back corner.

"Why don't you say hello to him?" Angela asked.

"He won't remember me," Jen said.

"He can't be that dumb," Angela said.

Jen got up and approached Lew Beach's table. He sipped dark wine as he peered at a folded newspaper through half-glasses.

"Mr. Beach?" she said. He looked up at her with a sharp expression that tempered slightly when he had studied her for a full minute.

"Oh," he said finally. "I thought it must be the waitress. College girl, eh? Art student?" He said "ott" for "art."

"I don't know if you remember me," she said. "I'm Jen Beckman. My aunt used to study with you. Kate Simon."

He smiled. "Of course. Titian hair. Bette Davis face. Lovely gal."

"She lives in Phoenix now," Jen said.

"I know," he said. "She writes to me; I call her now and then. Christmas cards, like that. You visited me a couple times. You remember what I said to you, first time we met?"

Jen, surprised, said "'Open your eyes. The mind will follow.'"

"Bright gal. The mind will follow and the heart. Don't forget the heart." *Hot.*

"Happiness too, you said."

"Happiness. Yeah. That too. Good seein' ya, kid. You've grown up nice."

As she turned to go, he added, "You know, I've always called her Kat, not Kate." Jen looked at him blankly, and he said, with a note in his voice that she could not interpret, "Just a little thing. Between us. Your aunt and me."

One day ten years later while home on vacation, Jen read in the *New York Times* that Lew Beach had died. The long obituary described his contributions to modern American painting. It named Raphael Soyer, Chirico, Hopper, Magritte, and the Group of Seven among the artists who had inspired him. Jen read the notice aloud to her parents as they ate Sunday breakfast on the back porch.

"'Though a close friend of Hilla Rebay and others of the non-objective school, Beach remained firmly committed to his own brand of realism that combined elements of—'"

"Skip all that art stuff," her father said.

Jen looked ahead for the paragraph that described Lew's birth to immigrant parents in New York, his education and early career. She read it aloud. The article went on: "'Beach was known for his bohemian lifestyle in Greenwich Village. He was a friend to artists in many fields, including Edna St. Vincent Millay, Jean Stafford, Walter Huston, George Balanchine—'"

"Does it mention Kate?" Maggie asked.

"Of course not," Jen said. "But it does say he taught at the Museum of Modern Art, NYU, and the New School—"

"The *New School!*" Maggie said. "I like that!"

"'He inspired many young artists, including—'"

"Never mind that," her father said. "When and where did he die?"

"'Beach died at his summer home in Sag Harbor,'" Jen read, "'where he has lived in seclusion since suffering a mental breakdown three years ago. He had—'" She stopped reading.

"Go on," Maggie said.

"It says he's been blind the last six years," Jen said.

"Hear that?" Maggie said, looking at her husband.

"Yeah," Dad said. His expression was gloomy.

"Didn't I tell you?" Maggie said. "Go on, Jen. Is there anything else?"

"The funeral arrangements. You planning on going?"

They laughed. But then Dad looked serious and said, "Better call Kate. She might want to go."

Aunt Kate flew in from Phoenix to attend the memorial service two weeks later. Then, she rode the train back to Goshen, took a cab to the house, and headed for the kitchen. She wore a black faille suit with a fitted jacket, a crisp black straw hat, black leather pumps. Without even taking off her hat, she drank tea with Jen and Maggie.

"Who was there?" Maggie asked.

"Nobody we know, except to read about. Actors, musicians, tons of artists. All in dreadful clothes. Hilla Rebay wore a lovely crushed-velvet suit. Two sizes too small, with egg down the front."

"What about Lew's family?" Maggie's tone was unreadable.

"His wife died years ago. I met his son Brendan. Nice guy. He's a lawyer in Connecticut. Lew left me a painting."

"You're in his will?" Maggie asked.

"No. He gave stuff to Brendan, with names tacked on. They'll ship the painting to me."

Jen saw the painting when she visited Aunt Kate a few years later, after Uncle Reg had died. It was small: only forty inches wide and twenty-five inches high. Aunt Kate hung it over the fireplace. Her living room had few furnishings and only two artifacts: a wrought-iron horse and the Beach painting. It aroused in Jen the same sense of alarm she had felt viewing his other paintings. There was a sky as high as Rousseau's *Carnival Night*, an emptiness as deep as a Chirico, yet the painting was full of people. The scene depicted was real in gorgeous detail; yet it was not real. Jen looked at the birds flecked into the upper-right corner and wondered if they were vultures. Aunt Kate saw her glance.

"You spotted the birds. There is a bird, or a group of birds, in every one of Lew's paintings. You ever notice?"

"No," Jen said. She stepped back, then said, "Banality and misery. That's what it represents. I don't mean that the painting is banal. The subject is. It's—"

"Ordinary," Aunt Kate said. She opened her mouth and with a delicate motion lifted a fleck of tobacco from her tongue. Jen had seen her make this same gesture hundreds of times. "The ordinary, that's what he liked. Plain people doing plain things. Drinking coffee around a salamander in the early morning, the sun coming up. Trucks with their lights on at dusk. People eating fried eggs and toast. Men sitting on girders."

Jen searched the picture. She could see distant buildings, a small shack in the foreground. The tiny human figures did not communicate with each other but seemed to appeal silently to the person viewing the painting. Dominating the whole scene was landscape and sky, in near-equal portions. The sky was especially terrifying. Jen shivered. "What's the title?" she asked.

"Paradisu," Aunt Kate said. "It has to do with simplicity. Aloneness."

"Nature looks so frightening. As if it could sweep all those little figures away."

"Nature has a habit of doing that," Aunt Kate said in her cigarette voice.

* * *

Aunt Kate achieved some fame on her own after moving to Phoenix. She acquired a following in outdoor art festivals, taught painting and drawing, had a few paintings bought by banks and small galleries, and even a one-woman show. She never knew fame as great as her teacher's, but like him she had a brief listing in the most recent edition of the same art directory in which Jen had looked up Lew Beach years before.

When Aunt Kate died, Jen inherited *Paradisu.* Maggie, visiting Jen and her husband for the Memorial Day weekend, looked at the painting with suspicion in her green eyes.

"What does it mean?" she asked.

"Come on, Ma. You're the one who always says you don't want to know what a thing means," Jen said.

"That's when I'm reading a book or a play," Maggie said. "Art is different."

"What does this painting look like to you?"

"A lot of people standing around in the wind."

"You know there's more to it than that."

"I know nothing of the sort. Except that it's depressing. Why do art and literature have to be so depressing all the time?"

"It's all in how you look at it," Jen said. "That picture you have over your piano—the Maxfield Parrish—"

"*The Garden of Allah*. Yes, I always liked that."

"This may surprise you, but the world isn't made up of lazy women in filmy garments lying around next to a pool somewhere in Araby. I call *that* depressing. Those women Parrish painted so carefully—they're slaves, Ma. Concubines. Worse than that, they're fake. They've no nipples or pubic hair."

"Rubbish," Maggie said and looked away from her. "What's the title of this painting, anyway?"

"Paradisu."

"Paradise? That?"

"Maybe the title's ironic. I'm not sure yet."

"Let me know when you figure it out. You know what he died of?" Maggie had a look of triumph in her eyes that made Jen wary.

"Lew Beach? No."

"Paresis. Syphilis. That's what you've inherited. And Kate—"

After a pause, Jen said, "Died of a pulmonary embolism."

"Ha! Well, she did smoke too much—and she was always frail—but I wonder. Remember the trouble she had with her back?"

"Arthritis. That's why she and Uncle Reg moved to Phoenix."

"*Maybe* it was arthritis. It—the other thing—never goes away, you know." Maggie's eyes were stones. "And remember she lost her baby—"

"Wait a minute. That was before she met Lew Beach. You've got your wars mixed up."

Maggie sighed. "I always worried after she took up with that man."

"You worried when she took up with Uncle Reg."

"Why couldn't she have married Oz McDonnell?" Maggie said. "He was prosperous, owned a feed store—she'd be alive today—"

"Don't rewrite history, Ma," Jen said.

Later, Jen looked at *Paradisu* more closely. The birds, Aunt Kate had said. There are birds in every painting. *Keep yer eyes open, kid.*

Some day, she thought, *I'll look up all his other paintings and hunt for the birds.*

The Art of It All

Tie it up and pull the strings tighter so the black will hold your breath for you
Just a quick inhalation and a pause of recognition
Not quite like waiting to be kissed; more like the moment before orgasm
But wrapping around your ribcage so tightly but not tightly enough never tightly enough
You pull the strings tighter and wish someone was standing behind you pulling the black strings until you swoon
And all the women before you breaking their ribs pulling on their corset strings to fit perfectly into the shape of someone else's desire
But it feels good to be held tight in this vise
Like when he pulled your hair and you submitted under a cascade of quickening pulses
His mouth on your neck, your hands on the kitchen counter, and
"Turn around," was all he growled, low and hungry
And as you stand in front of the mirror and pull the damn thing tighter
you suddenly release and
The strings glide through your fingers and dance along your back
And go slack against your body like the reins of a rider who's given up

Frozen Puberty

Maureen would make me play this game. It was one of those board games called "Build An Empire." The board was a map of the world and each player got all these little wooden cubes that would be armies. You would start off with a bunch of armies and countries and try to invade all the other countries and take over the world. The battles were decided by the toss of dice. I really hated the game because the only way it could end was by someone getting completely smashed off the board. As soon as one player got the edge over the other his chances of winning increased like crazy. I think it's called having the odds increase geometrically or something. Because as he got new territories his armies would grow like mad, the logic being that the people in these areas changed sides.

If I was really winning I'd look at my cubes all over the board and feel sorry for Maureen. Like let's say I had the green cubes and she had the purple ones; after the game changed in my favor the board would be all green with just a few purple cubes. And Maureen was so great about losing. She'd hole up in some nonsense place like Ethiopia and start talking to her remaining armies like they were old friends, urging them to hold on. Once someone was down they could never recover and I'd always say, "Ah, let's quit now, you're not getting out of Ethiopia." But she'd sort of stick out her face and say "Come in and get me." It was really a crummy game. I hate having to get creamed or having to cream someone.

After a while she started beating me regularly. Maureen thought it was because she was mastering the strategy of the game. The real reason she started winning was that I would try to lengthen the middle part of the game. The middle part was really interesting. That was when both players were matched even and changes made on the board were slow but important. If I had a chance to rush in and start to take over, I'd sort of go in slow so I could watch the game turn slowly in my favor. This never worked because it gave Maureen a chance to redefend her weak areas and then find an opening and attack me. The middle part was okay, but I wish there was a way to stay at it and avoid the shitty ending.

Maybe I just hated the game because Maureen made me play it before we necked. It was always the same. I'd come in and her folks would be in the hall putting on their coats. Me and Maureen would say things like "enjoy the show" and like that. And her father's and my eyes would sort of meet, like him knowing that all we're going to do is play "Build An Empire," then neck a little. I wished he'd look worried like I was a big lover and sex fiend, but he just says, "Sure you don't want to join us now? I hear it's a good movie; plenty of hippies. Oh well, have a good time." Having a girl's father look at you the way girls' fathers look at me doesn't do much for your confidence.

We'd watch them leave; her dad was always careful to help Maureen's mom if there was ice on the driveway. Her mom was pregnant. Maureen would have a much younger sister or brother soon. She had an older sister who was also having a baby. This sister, Moira, lived in Canada and Maureen was the only one in the family she spoke to. They had a code. Maureen would call Canada long distance, let it ring once, and then hang up. This meant the house was empty and Moira would call back.

There were a lot of Friday and Saturday nights that I spent in that house holding Maureen's hand and hearing half of their conversations. The big joke was whether or not Moira's kid would be born before or after the New York baby. Once Maureen explained to me how an aunt or uncle could be younger than their niece or nephew. I didn't get it at first but she lined up some wooden cubes from "Build An Empire," and showed me the generation stuff. I could do it for you.

Anyway. Her folks would leave and I'd follow Maureen down the narrow paneled staircase and she'd get her call and then set up our game. Walking behind her was great. She really is beautiful. Really.

Walking behind her you could see her figure and how it kept moving. Not back and forth like the sexy ladies in the movies, but up and down going down the steps. Shit, you'd have to see her to know how perfect she was. And I'm such a crumb going down the stairs thinking how lucky I am.

Maureen was so hot. She'd gone out with guys with cars and everything. All her friends thought that she was nuts to mess around with a crumb like me. Her friends were always asking to get her older brother (a guy I stocked shelves with) to set them up with some seniors. Maureen told them to fuck-off.

Her friends once played one of the best practical jokes on me. It was a classic and I fell for it all the way. This Betty (a real dog who's always supposed to be going on double dates with us, but then her date never shows and Maureen makes her drag along with us) calls me and says I'd better *"Start packing."* and *"Head for the hills!"*

This Betty says some guy named Francis just got out of the Navy and heard about me and Maureen and was coming over to kill me because he was an old boyfriend. I didn't believe it at first but then this Betty starts giving me all these facts. She said Francis just got sent back from an aircraft carrier off Vietnam that had caught fire. He'd won some kind of medal for dragging guys out of the kitchen, but had gotten his face all burnt and went a little crazy.

An aircraft carrier had caught fire a while ago and this Betty was telling the story real good. She kept saying how tough and crazy Francis was. Francis? If Betty was making this up the guy would have a name like Spike or Hank. It sounds stupid, but I bought it. I pictured a guy with purple scars and a Navy uniform covered with medals beating me up in front of my parents. I took the Long Island Railroad to my cousin's house. We dug clams all weekend. My aunt made sauce and skinny macaroni.

When I got back the whole school was laughing at me. You can really tell who your friends are when the whole world is laughing at you. Your friends laugh in your face real loud. They call you a jerk and punch you in the shoulder. The crumbs sort of sulk around and grin like they hate your guts and the reason they hate you is because you're so stupid falling for a joke like that. And it's their duty to go around hating stupid jerks. I took everybody giving me the business pretty well.

Maureen laughed in my face real loud. She called me a jerk, punched me in the shoulder and then rubbed and kissed the spot she punched. The next time we had our routine date over her house, she let me do other stuff besides our usual necking. You can never tell when Maureen is going to let you do other stuff. She does now and then and it drives me wild. And other times she'd refused to do stuff again. I always say that if we did it before we can do it again. But Maureen never figures this way.

I don't know what she was thinking the week after the made-up Francis didn't kill me. We were in her basement and she was talking to her sister in Canada. I heard half the conversation the way you do when you're with someone on the phone.

"How ya' feeling, Moira? …"

"Mom's as big as a house … I says do you want it to be a girl or a boy and she says she wants it to be over … you guys could have babies on the same day …Yeah, yeah, yeah, I'd be a big sister, little sister, aunt and sex animal all on the same day. Lotta balls in the air for the Maureen*ster!"*

"Nah, I'm not alone I'm with that guy who works at the A&P with Bad Brother Billy. .. ."

I stood there and heard Maureen tell the story about how the made-up Francis didn't kill me. I was a little annoyed that Maureen didn't say my name.

"What are *we doing*? Ya' know … what would you do if the tribe was out and you had the house? We're playing *The White Album, we're* playing the crappy war game the Dad*ster says* will teach me geography … Nah, we still can't say your name in the house."

I was annoyed that she didn't tell Moira my name. But I wasn't annoyed when she dropped her pants, took my hand and turned it sideways between her legs and rode it.

"What are we doing? We're doing shit that can't fuck you up and get you pregnant!"

She got on her knees.

"And I'm sorry but I can't talk on the long distance when my mouth is full!"

She hung up. This beat the shit out of "Build An Empire." The little wooden army-cubes stayed in the box that night.

There was an ice storm on the next Friday night and I was worried that her folks wouldn't be able to get out. But it was their Civil War Discussion Night, and the old man wouldn't miss that. Her mother sat on a little stool in the hall and struggled with her tight rubber boots. One of her boots got away and I picked it up. I bent over close and when I handed it to her I whispered, "The North wins, stay home tonight." I don't remember if I meant it. But even now I remember her smile.

They left. The icy driveway was tough for them, but they got better traction by working together. We went to the basement steps, there was a brother or two home because of the storm, but "The Squealer" was out.

For a while I looked to see if there would be any carry-over from the big night we had last week. I never say shit to the guys like, "I dropped a load on her tonsils," but I felt like talking like that to Maureen. We could talk that way together. I hinted around a little.

Last week didn't seem to affect Maureen at all. Her conversation with her sister went as usual. The Beatles sounded the same, and she began setting up the crummy game. You know I was thinking about how the top of her head looked last week when she made the *'talking with her mouthful'* joke with Moira up in Canada. We played "Build An Empire."

I had the yellow armies and the cards gave me most of North America and a lot of Russia. If the dice just let me win a few early battles I could join my forces by using the little connection on the board at the Bering Strait. It could be a fast win for me. Maureen had the purple cubes, her armies were spread out and that put her at a disadvantage. We rolled the dice. I won like three tosses in a row and got more territories and more wooden armies. I was at the Bering Strait. Maureen got the tight smile she gets when she concentrates. She began to talk to her armies. She lost a few more battles.

I steered away from the Bering Strait. I knew I could make this game last forever if she would just win a few tosses and concentrated on coming straight up the Mississippi River. She did just that and we were locked in a stalemate. Her spirits picked up when she saw she had an even chance of winning. She began to get a looser smile, and went upstairs to get two sodas. I knew she also wanted to check on the number of brothers drifting around and make sure "The Squealer" was still out.

She came down with two glasses of Coke and ice; I heard her latch the door. I lost about eight dice tosses in a row and the game ended. I turned the lights out and started grabbing Maureen and she started grabbing me. It was our usual necking with our clothes on.

I'm a crumb and everything, but someone hot like Maureen grabbing at me in the dark makes me feel like a real hotshot. When we were necked-out she turned on the lights and we saw that the ice in the soda was all melted. You couldn't drink the soda anymore because it was watered down and warm. Sitting there the glasses weren't good looking but I had to look at them because of the shades of brown. Before the Coke was all brown with dullish white cubes floating in it. But now there was this slow and well-defined change in colors from Coke-brown to water-white. It wasn't cool looking like before and I was really thirsty from all that necking. Maureen was always too fast at running upstairs and dumping the glasses out and getting some more soda. I like to look at the warm glasses while I was real dry and my mouth feeling kind of numb. I didn't tell Maureen that or she'd think I was nuts.

Maureen almost let me go all the way with her on one of our last real dates. It was early in the spring but the temperature was really high for that time of year. We decided to go the whole route with a bottle of whiskey and a picnic lunch. We hitched to the beach. It was great being out in the sun with Maureen (her being mostly a winter girlfriend). Our ride let us off and we started walking towards the ocean.

The path changed from dirt to a dirt and sand mixture, and then to pure sand. There's this one spot on a sand dune that's almost a hill in some spots where you can sort of be at the beach and in the little woods north of the beach, all at the same time.

I like that spot a lot. I told Maureen we should spread our blanket there. She didn't like that spot at all. She said we should either go down to the beach or back in the grass and trees, but not right there on the path. I couldn't force her to stay there. We walked back and sat under some small trees.

We ate and were surprised at how good the whiskey tasted. Maureen talked, I listened, and it started getting all sexy. We reached the point where she always made me stop and kept on going. Then we were naked. We were breathing like crazy. Maureen was on her back but she seemed to be flying up as she pulled me down like I was sinking into her. Her mouth was deep and the only thing I could do with my hands was hold her head. Finally we're all ready and she says something about me not having a scum bag. I was all for going ahead because I couldn't picture Maureen ever being pregnant. But she says something about not wanting to move to Canada. The right moment sort of passed.

Hitching home I tried to notice a change, like her being romantic or acting more mature or something. But she was the same Maureen.

We started having a lot of fights. Always asking each other *"What's the matter?"* which is the dumbest thing to say when you're fighting with someone. Our dates changed, we didn't play "Build An Empire." I would be with my friends early on summer nights while she smoked pot with her meatball friends. We usually met after midnight. We had the whiskey and the blanket. I never had a scum bag. Maureen knew I never would have one. Then I just didn't call her anymore.

Walter, my best friend, started going out with Maureen and really fucking her. It was the fall of our senior year and about a week after I broke up with Maureen I did have sex with one of his sister's friends from Seaford High. So it was sort of great both of us not being virgins.

But Walter was a virgin longer than me, on account of Maureen acting real prudy with him at first. He told me that Maureen did a lot of crying and stuff when I dumped her. It was hard to believe, me being such a crumb and everything. He asked me how come I stopped seeing her. And I was going to explain to him how she didn't like that spot on the path and everything. I was going to tell him how it was either woods or beach for Maureen. But didn't. But didn't because I thought Walter was changing into a real crumb.

Immolation

You were always a
conflagration,
ego and valour clashing
impossibly.
I was young and
did not yet recognize
the nobility
in how you hold
the line of your shoulders.
But what life of mine
could not come to revolve
around you? You,
I know now,
the once and future.

Single Memphis

Josey hadn't been with a man in almost a year. She'd been pregnant at fifteen and then again at eighteen. She'd given both up for adoption. After that, she'd doubled up—condoms and birth control; that did the trick for a couple of years. It kept her from getting pregnant, anyway, but it didn't do a damn thing to keep her from choosing the wrong man. Josey was twenty-one now and celibate. She'd gotten good at gettin' none, she liked to say.

Jefferson Davis made Josey sing a different tune the day he walked into the Tigermart looking for a Blue Freeze slushie and a 5-hour Energy drink. He was a cop, and Josey generally held a low opinion of Memphis cops, but she just smiled at this one. He was tall, with barely-there muscles that peeked out from the short sleeves of his shirt and smooth black skin, a shaved bald head she knew would feel like silk against her cheek when she held him in bed. They talked, and she watched as the slushie turned his tongue a deeper and deeper blue the longer the conversation went on. He showed up at the Tigermart almost every morning after that.

A few weeks after she'd first seen Jefferson, Josey had lunch with her friend Martha. They shared a plate of barbeque pork nachos and drank Bud Light out of plastic cups on the patio behind The Barbeque Shop. The plastic sweated and slipped in Josey's hand, and she felt her skin flush under the late August sun. The humidity made everything damp; Martha's curls were wild with frizz. Josey reached out and smoothed a curl down, smiled at Martha, then asked for help.

"What to do with a girl like Josey," Martha said.

"I like him," Josey said.

"You like every boy. That's just what you do." Martha shrugged.

"Jefferson's not a boy, though. He's gotta be at least twenty-six." Josey licked her fingers clean. "He likes me, too. I know it. You shoulda seen him. He set me on fire."

"It's not fair. I can't find a boy to take me to dinner in the whole of U-Memphis, but you can just pick them out of line at the Tigermart."

"Maybe you're the lucky one," Josey said. "Boys only lead to trouble." She thought of a thumbnail small as an ant, of pursed little duck lips, all she could picture of her second son. The first was a complete blank; she'd been too far gone on pain, hadn't even wanted to see it. "Maybe hot cop should just stay a fantasy."

"You just gotta be careful. You could get your tubes tied. That's what my mom did after she had me."

"Nuh-uh," Josey said. "I want to have babies eventually."

"You've had babies."

"Yeah, but I wanna keep one."

* * *

Josey sometimes watched the college kids while she stood behind her cash register, especially this time of year when the schools were starting to fill up again. Her Tigermart was situated at the corner of Poplar and McLean, and there were three colleges nearby. Josey could have had that, she knew. Her high school counselor had told her she was smart enough, but she didn't have the grades; she wasn't getting scholarships to anywhere. She wanted to go to college, though, maybe do a nursing program. So she worked. And she saved.

Josey was working the morning shift as usual when a couple of college kids walked in. One poked around the refrigerated section, loaded his arms with sodas and bottles of vitamin water. The other looked at the egg sandwiches wrapped in their red and white checked wrapping. Josey had just put them in the warming bins a few minutes before. She wondered how Jefferson took his eggs. She wouldn't mind making him a breakfast that didn't come out of a microwave. Her grandma had taught her how to make homemade biscuits and cheese grits with shrimp when she was just a little girl, and Josey's least complicated and most favorite fantasy consisted of serving a man she'd just pleased in bed her grandma's best recipes.

The first kid walked up to her counter and put his drinks down. He wore a shirt with "Habitat for Humanity" faded across his chest. When he looked at her, his eyes were bloodshot. He said "hello" then collapsed in front of her.

"Oh," Josey said. She walked around the front of her counter, kneeled and put a hand to the boy's chest. She didn't feel it move. She looked at his friend. "I don't think he's breathing."

The friend sunk to the floor, sat cross-legged. He pulled a cell phone out of his pocket and called 911.

"Do you know CPR?" Josey said.

"We should stay calm," he said. He explained to the person on the phone where they were and what had happened. He looked at Josey. "The lady on the phone says we should try to do CPR while we wait."

"Okay," Josey said.

"I don't know how." He scooted on his butt toward them until his knee touched Josey's leg.

Josey thought she knew. She took the phone from the boy, tucked it between her ear and shoulder, and listened as the voice on the other end talked her through the steps. The Tigermart floor was greasy beneath her bare knees. She pinched the boy's nose shut and pressed her lips to his. His mouth wasn't open; he wasn't responsive, so she had to tug at his chin a bit, though it was stiff as if he'd clenched his teeth. It reminded her of in high school when they'd dissected a baby pig and had to break its jaw. Though she didn't remember why, she remembered sticking her thumb in the pig's mouth and tugging. Josey shivered. She blew a breath in the boy's mouth then sat up, folded her hands over where she thought his heart might be, did five chest compressions, then did the whole thing over again.

She felt hands on her shoulders and the phone fell to the ground as she was pulled away. It was Jefferson, come for his Slushie. He took over for her, pumped and pumped until the ambulance showed and the EMT tried the paddles. In the end, the kid was dead.

Josey waited outside with the other boy while they loaded his friend on a stretcher. A man walked up, scuffing across the brown grass between the sidewalk and parking lot, and complained at her about not being able to buy his cigarettes. Josey flipped him off and asked him if he didn't have an ounce of respect in his body.

The boy watched her. She felt her face heat a bit when she turned back to him.

"Am I supposed to go to the hospital now?" the boy asked. "Is that how this works?"

"I don't know. Maybe you should call his family?"

"He doesn't have any here. He's not from Memphis."

"Do you know how to get in touch with them?"

"He's only been my roommate for two weeks." He smiled a little.

"What's your name?"

"Mike," the kid said. "I liked him."

Josey squeezed his hand. Jefferson stepped up just then. "You two all right?"

"Mike here isn't quite sure what to do. Maybe you could help him some?"

"I don't know his family," Mike said.

"That's okay. You give me his name and what you do know and we'll get in touch with who matters."

Josey went back to work, though she squinted through the spaces between the Pall Mall and Coke ads hung in the windows and watched while Mike and Jefferson talked. After a time, Jefferson held the passenger door to his squad car open for Mike. Jefferson got in on the other side. They left.

The next day was Josey's day off. She woke early, her body not used to sleeping much past five a.m., though it wasn't late enough in the year for that to mean she woke in the dark. She was grateful for that. Come November, she'd trek to work in the dark and slouch home in the dark and she'd feel so depressed at only seeing the sun through a dirty window covered in signs that she'd start to think about how this wasn't her life. Maybe it was time to move on to something new. But that wasn't possible yet, and those thoughts only complicated things, so she was grateful for the days she had without them.

She ate toast and grape jelly at the kitchen counter, squinting into the dusty light. She listened to her mom who was on the couch in the next room, muttering in her sleep. Some nights her mom made it to bed; some she didn't. Her mom had tried to be a lawyer once, but it didn't pan out. She was a paralegal, and Josey thought she was okay with the position. Mom liked her alcohol, though. She drank Ice Picks—sweet tea and vodka—and Josey suspected she started at lunch most days. Ice Picks and all, Josey felt a devotion to her mom. She'd kept a roof over Josey's head, and she'd put all her extra money into sending Josey to private school to get her away from those damn city schools that weren't worth a shit.

Her mom hadn't been mad the first time Josey came home pregnant, but she'd sat in their kitchen for a long time, hands clenched over her knees. When she'd finally walked back into the living room, there was a run in her RiteAid pantyhose where one of her nails had caught the fabric. She didn't chastise Josey, just offered to help her out if she'd wanted to get an abortion. But Josey didn't want that. She thought maybe she didn't deserve to take such an easy way out. Better for her to have nine months of a reminder, to work to make sure the baby had a good home. Better to teach herself that lesson. Not that it took, considering she was pregnant again a couple years later.

Josey brushed her toast crumbs into the sink and looked around the kitchen. She was restless. There were some old bananas sitting on the microwave, peels spotted black-brown. Josey grabbed the bunch and peeled them one by one and put them in a bowl. She mashed them with a fork. She grabbed her grandma's recipe book down from on top of the refrigerator, then she made banana bread. She put chocolate chips in it for good measure.

While the loaves baked, Josey got dressed. She put on a jean skirt, long enough to avoid what Martha called "slut syndrome" but short enough to show some leg, and she curled long, loose ringlets into her red hair. She knew when she wore it like that instead of in the ponytail she always wore at work, her face looked soft and round, and she could get any guy to turn his eyes her way.

Josey pulled the bread out of the oven and set it on a rack to cool. She shook her mom awake and got her up and sitting at the kitchen table with a cup of coffee. Mom yawned around a "Good morning," then sprawled on the table, all elbows and long limbs like a teenager.

"What's the occasion, Josey baby?" she said.

"I think maybe I met someone," Josey said.

"This someone gonna be trouble?"

"They always are." Josey grinned. She sliced the bread. She'd never brought a man baked goods before. She wanted it to look nice on the plate.

"I'm serious."

"No, momma. It ain't like that. He's sweet. He's a cop."

"Well good. Cause all cops got good morals." Her mom raised an eyebrow.

"That ain't fair."

"You just be careful."

Josey smiled. "I'm gonna woo him today."

"Oh, Josey." Her mom's mouth wobbled and she hid it behind her coffee.

Josey went to the police station at what she hoped was the end of Jefferson's shift. She knew from their morning talks he worked long days and he had to drop his cruiser off before going home. She perched on a low concrete wall that ran around the building, lifted her face into the sun and kicked her legs while she waited for him, the bread in neat slices on a platter in her lap. Half an hour or so later, Jefferson stepped outside and Josey hopped down.

"Josey?" he said. He tilted his head to the side, his eyes wrinkled in the corners as he smiled a little. "What're you doing here?"

"I wanted to say thanks," Josey said. She held the plate in front of her. "For what you did yesterday."

“It was my job. Besides, you did just as much. You coulda saved his life. You coulda been a real hero.” He stepped closer. “Seemed like you knew what you were doing.”

“I took a few babysitting classes when I was a teenager. They make you get certified to do CPR. In case a kid falls in a pool, or something.”

“Or something,” Jefferson agreed.

He still hadn’t taken the plate. “Here,” Josey said. “Banana bread. It makes good peanut butter and jelly sandwiches.”

He took it from her. Josey bit her lip, wanting to sigh at the way his hands were big enough to dwarf the plate.

“Hey,” he said. “You wanna have dinner?”

* * *

It was weeks later when Josey decided she was in love with Jefferson. She and Martha were at the movies. It was an old theater, the kind that didn’t even have stadium seating and that really fat people were uncomfortable in because the seats were too small. It was the first week of October, and the theater was playing Night of the Living Dead. They would play a horror movie classic each night leading up to Halloween, and Josey knew she and Martha would see at least one a week. Jefferson wasn’t interested. He said he saw enough horror on the job, which Josey secretly rolled her eyes at because she was pretty sure he just dealt with crack addicts and prostitutes, no blood or guts at all.

Josey ate a handful of popcorn. Her palm was buttery. Had they been kids, she would have wiped it on Martha’s shirt to gross her out. She wiped it on a napkin instead and set her popcorn on the floor.

“I think this is good for me,” Josey whispered. “It’s like a real, mature relationship.”

“That’s good, girlie.” Martha slid down in her seat, propped her feet up on the chair in front of her, and looked up at Josey. “I think that’s good for you.”

Josey agreed. She did. But the problem was, they hadn’t had sex. Not once in a month. Jefferson wanted to wait. Josey didn’t want to scare him off, and she knew it was probably good to continue her no sex streak, but she didn’t understand it. She was used to boys who wanted to grope her in the backseat before they'd even gotten to the date part of the date. She was used to fast and dirty. She was used to rough. She liked it that way.

The night before, Jefferson had pulled her into his bed and held her. He'd run one of his big hands through her hair and he'd said her name and she'd felt so cherished she'd wanted to cry. They'd made out with long, slow kisses, and Jefferson had touched every part of her body except for where it really mattered.

Josey had woken in his bed that morning and she'd watched him sleep. She'd touched with light fingers the bridge of his nose, his morning stubble, his shoulder blades. She liked how pronounced they were while he slept, always on his stomach. He was thin. She could see his ribs if he stretched the right way. She touched the bare skin just behind his ear. He'd told her he'd had dreads once, but he'd shaved them down when he'd become a cop. It was better anyway, he'd said. He'd said a black man with dreads has more problems than most. She didn't know what he meant, exactly, but she believed him.

He opened his eyes at the feel of her fingers. "That tickles," he'd said. "Feels like cobwebs brushing on my skin."

"Maybe I'm a spider."

He smiled.

"Brown recluse."

"Naw," he said. "You ain't that dangerous."

"Maybe I am," she said. "Maybe you should be scared of me." She gripped his bicep, tugged him, nudged at him until he was flipped over and she crawled on top, straddled across his thighs. She slid her hands up his arms until she held his wrists above his head. "I wanna break you."

He smirked at her. "You could try."

She pressed a hand to his crotch. He was almost hard beneath his boxers. He lost his smirk. "Don't," he said.

"I'll make it good. Don't you want that?"

Jefferson tugged his hands free and pushed her to the bed. He sat up. "Just," he said. His fingers twitched. "I want it. But sex ain't easy for me."

Josey went to her knees, the tips of her fingers pressed into the bed sheets. "Why not?" she said.

"Do we have to talk about this now? I gotta get ready for work."

"You got an hour."

"You keeping tabs on my schedule?"

Josey smiled and looked away. "Maybe."

"That's cute."

Josey wouldn't be derailed. "It's not normal," she said. "I never met a man before who didn't want to come if it was on offer."

"Jesus."

"Is it," Josey paused. She waved her hand through the air. "You're all right down there?"

Jefferson shook his head. "Everything works." He was angry now. Josey tightened her grip on the sheets. "I guess I just thought, with what you told me about your past, sex might not be easy for you, too."

"All right." She pressed her palm to his chest. "It's all right," she'd said.

"What do you think it is?" Josey said now, looking down at Martha who was still slouched in her seat. Josey could make out the details of her face only occasionally, when the theater screen brightened for an instant.

"Dunno," Martha said.

"It ain't that important, right?" Josey said. "Sex?"

Martha shrugged. "I wouldn't know."

Josey shoved her shoulder a bit. "You'll get there. You just gotta stop hanging out with me all the damn time. Let's go home, huh? We've seen this one. And Jefferson said he'd call."

* * *

At the Tigermart the next day, Josey flipped through an issue of "Single Memphis" she'd stolen from the floorboard of Martha's car. It was a cheap newsprint 'zine she and Martha used to make fun of when they were in high school, though she'd seen Martha with them on more than one occasion since then. It ran pages of ads for dating services and features on the most eligible singles in Memphis. Jefferson told her he'd been featured once, when he was only twenty-two. She wondered if she'd been pregnant when he'd put himself out there for all of Memphis. She did the math. When he was twenty-two, she would have been fifteen—pregnant and boy crazy and in love with the world anyway. She smiled at the thought. She wondered if he still had a copy.

She was drawing hearts in the corners of every page and wondering why Jefferson wouldn't go all the way when Mike walked in. Or Mike with the Dead Friend, as she thought of him in that moment.

"You remember me?" he said.

Josey nodded. "You need some gas?"

"No. Are you busy?"

"I'm working."

They both looked around at the empty store.

"Yeah," he said.

"Sorry," she said. "I'm real sorry about what happened with your friend."

"Thanks," he said.

"Nothing to thank me for."

"That's actually why I came," he said. "I sort of froze when it happened. But you tried to help. So thanks."

"Sure."

Mike put his hands in his pockets.

"You want a Coke or something?" Josey said. She walked to the fountain.

"All right."

She grabbed a cup.

"Lots of ice," he said.

"Coming right up."

When she handed him the Coke, he was smiling at her and playing with the blow pops set along side the register. "I should be the one buying you a Coke."

"You see me get out any money? Just don't tell any of the other customers. They'll be jealous."

She walked behind her counter and leaned against it, chin propped on her palm, elbow against the hard plastic that covered the ads spread atop the counter. "Did they ever find out what happened? With your friend?"

"Aneurism."

"Yikes."

"I know."

"That's scary," she said. He leaned against the counter from the other side. She touched his shoulder.

A customer walked in and they pulled apart.

"Thirty on pump two," the customer said. He tugged his pants up by the belt, though not enough to cover his boxers. He threw a twenty and a ten on the counter.

"Gotcha," Josey said. She set the pump from the register and put the money in her drawer. She leaned against the counter again.

"It's just weird," Mike said, after a time. "I didn't know him all that well, and I sort of just keep picturing him like that. Dead like that, lying on the floor. I can't picture him alive, like at all." He shrugged. "It's weird."

"My daddy died when I was little," Josey said. "I was ten. I can only picture him in his coffin."

"That sucks."

"Yeah."

"The guys in my dorm keep coming to my room. They've stopped asking me what it was like, but now I'm the only one with a room to myself. I can't decide if I like them hanging around all the time or if I just want to scream. I want the privacy. I guess it's kind of shitty of me to be happy I have my own room, huh?"

"Well, you didn't know him."

"Yeah."

Another customer came in.

"I better go," Mike said. "Class."

"Yeah," Josey said. He walked out the door and across the lot. Josey watched until he rounded the corner. She rang up the new customer's Mountain Dew and microwave burrito.

* * *

Josey let herself into Jefferson's apartment that night. She'd gotten paid that day, so she'd gone to Kroger first to get groceries. Now she set everything out on Jefferson's counters and went about the business of making her grandma's chicken and dumplings. Josey had been eating these same dumplings since she'd had teeth.

It was dark out by the time Jefferson got home. The food was simmering on the stove, and Josey was lying on Jefferson's couch with a copy of the Jefferson issue of "Single Memphis."

Jefferson grinned, lopsided like he was embarrassed. He shook his head. "Where'd you find that, Joz?

"Under your bed. You take it out and look at it now and again? Dream of what you used to be?"

"Nope. I got everything I need right here. That kid? He doesn't exist no more." He leaned over her, kissed her right between the eyes. He slid the magazine from her hand and dropped it on the floor.

"I like the dreads." She cupped the back of his head with her hand. "I like this better."

He put both hands in her hair, straddled her so that they were both on the couch.

"You cooked," he said.

"Uh huh."

"You make me crazy, I love you so much."

"Is that what you were looking for when you posed for that picture? Someone to cook you dinner?"

"Maybe. What about you? What were you looking for when you slept with all those boys?"

Josey stilled. "Jefferson."

"I don't like thinking about you with them. I don't like thinking you had someone else's babies first."

Josey sat up. Jefferson followed. He looked at the magazine on the floor.

"So don't think about it," Josey said.

"I can't help it." He laughed a little. He scratched the nape of his neck. "I been thinking about you all day."

"I'm right here."

"I've heard that before."

Josey cradled the back of his head in her hand. She rubbed her thumb behind his ear. "What's going on in here," she said.

Jefferson shook his head.

"You can talk to me. You just nervous, or something? Are you a virgin?" Josey half whispered the last word, like it was dirty.

"No." Jefferson pulled away. "I've been having sex since I was fourteen."

"All right," Josey said.

Jefferson rubbed a hand across his mouth, glanced at her sideways. "My first was my momma's friend," he said. "She was thirty-two, I think, older than me." He dragged his shoe along the carpet. "I used to let her tie me up. Do things to me." He shrugged. "When I told her I loved her for real she laughed at me. Left me tied to my own bed for my dad to find."

Josey wanted to touch him again but kept her hands to herself. "What happened?" she said.

"It doesn't matter. You're mine, right Josey? You and me? This is real?"

Josey hoped so. She'd started to feel like she had a plan now. Jefferson. College. No more Tigermart, and no more Mom's apartment.

"Of course, baby," she said.

* * *

Mike started showing up at the Tigermart regular—for an hour or so between or after classes and all day on Fridays. Sometimes he read the newspapers and dollar paperbacks that never got sold, but most of the time Josey let him hang out behind the counter with her, let him spread out and work on his homework as long as he didn't get in her way.

Three weeks into this new thing between the two of them, Josey felt restless. Mike was perched on a stool behind her, a pen cap in his mouth, ink on his hands—he was a lefty, and while writing, he had a habit of smearing his words behind him as his hand moved across the page. His eyes were on Josey instead of his books. Josey knew he watched her. She noticed it the very first time he'd just hung around without talking. She knew what he wanted, too. He wasn't any different from any other boy.

Josey wanted him to watch her. Fridays, she spent all day feeling his eyes roaming between his books and her body, her face, and she went home to Jefferson so horny that their no sex situation was making her feel like she would strangle someone. Jefferson knew, and he tried. He made her come with his hands and his mouth, but he wouldn't let Josey reciprocate, and he wouldn't give her what she really wanted. Josey wanted him inside of her. Josey wanted to consume him.

Josey felt Mike watching her and it was too much. She turned to him. "What are you staring at?"

"Sorry," Mike said. He looked back at his notes. He smiled.

Josey leaned against the counter. "You like me, Mike?" she said.

"You know I do, Josey."

"Yeah, but I mean, do you *like* me, like me?"

"Yeah, I *like* you, like you."

"You wanna fuck me?"

Mike's smile dropped. He turned back to his work, flipped a page in his notes. "Yes," he almost whispered.

"I thought so." Josey turned around. Mike watched her for another minute then packed up and left.

He came back the next day at the end of her shift. They stood in the parking lot together.

"How did you think this would work?" Josey said.

Mike shrugged. He leaned against the trunk of his car. "I didn't really think it would. That's not the only reason I've been coming to see you. I guess I thought we could be friends. But if you want? Maybe we could be more."

"I've got a boyfriend."

"That cop, right? He's cool. He was really helpful that day."

"That's Jefferson for you."

"You two are like," he waved a hand through the air, "serious, or whatever?"

Josey caught his hand. She turned into him, tilted her face up, kissed him on the lips. "Yeah," she said. "We're serious."

"Oh."

Mike followed her home, their cars like hitched train cars he tailgated her so closely. Josey's mom wasn't home yet, and they stumble-walked to the sofa, kissing and groping as they went. Josey shoved Mike down and crawled on top of him. They had sex, fast and rough. Mike's cock was inside her almost before she could get her underwear off, foreplay obviously a foreign concept, and when she felt him come inside of her, it was too early, and she hadn't even gotten any pleasure out of it.

"Sorry," he said when it was over. He touched her shoulder. "Sorry, Josey."

"It's okay," she said.

Mike left, and Jefferson called hours later. Josey didn't answer. She sat in the kitchen and she cried.

She and Martha went to the movies together the next day. Afterwards, the parking lot was filled with wind and fallen, blowing leaves. Josey hugged herself against the chill. She was wearing one of Jefferson's jackets, and she tucked it against her chin. She looped her arm with Martha's; they leaned against each other as they walked.

"You think I'm screwed up?" Josey asked. She hoped her words would blow away with the wind.

"What do you want me to say to that, Josey?"

Tell the truth, Josey wanted to say, but she already knew what that was. She shrugged instead.

Martha, her fingertips chilled, wrapped her hand around Josey's.

When Martha dropped Josey at home, Josey went inside and laid in the dark. She listened to the wind and the rush of leaves tapping against her window. She listened to her mom snoring in the next room. She listened to the absence of Jefferson's breathing beside her. In just the couple of months they'd been together, she'd already gotten used to that sound. She liked sleeping with him. It meant actually sleeping. It meant pillows and blankets and bodies, warm and heavy, wrapped together until there were dreams, and it meant waking up together and blinking bleary-eyed across the bed until one of them smiled.

She gathered herself and a few things and drove to Jefferson's. She used the key he kept under the cracked sun tea jug on the porch and snuck in. He was home, asleep on his stomach, the blankets kicked off. Josey stripped. She ran a hand up his calf. He jumped, waking suddenly, and she smiled when he looked back at her.

"Hey, Joz," he said.

"Hey," she said.

She crawled onto the bed, lifted his arm, and tucked herself beneath. She pressed her nose to his skin.

The Little Beauties

The Bridesmaids drape on furniture like Botticelli's tired women, waiting to pose—sad and bored faces in their pastel blues—it's the fourth wedding this year, and one more morning glass of champagne at the hair salon will simply kill them—though it gives a sexy droopiness to their eyes—eyes that water for the camera, twinkle for the men, cry for the bride—another one gone to the White Dress, matching appliances, wineglasses to die for, and 7 beautifully photographed days in Paris—but now on this auspicious day, they celebrate, because they are almost sure this is what they want too.

Erogeneity/Etiology

Too timid to stare, the writer looks the leggy blonde over quickly and returns to page three of her story. Projected onto the page, the snapshot captured the tall stranger, possibly with a tattoo on her chest, leaning over the bar to charm the bartender. The writer hears the stranger laugh. The bartender hasn't told a joke. She only expected him to.

The story Emily is writing doesn't utilize monsters, killers, or violence. She wants to institute a new genre of fiction she calls "existential horror." She also calls it *existentialist horror.* One sounds better than the other. She hasn't determined which.

Emily has nothing against writing monsters, but a good monster is the reification of a good idea, and horror writers finished with all the good ideas in the 1980s. She could build a monster around an existing idea, but *going retro* leaves her feeling cheap, and for the same reason she doesn't like pirating music. Downloading four gigs of songs *just because* misses the value of music—and impersonal imitation misses the value of creation. Stealing doesn't offend her. When Kathy Acker plagiarized, she made what she stole hers. The offense is doing for the sake of doing, is getting for the sake of having.

Emily's unnamed story is supposed to depict the universal dread of solitary interior existence amid the atmosphere of a genre horror story. So far the story depicts a petty argument between a couple in their early twenties. Male fails to connect with female on the symbolic level. Men require longer wavelengths to distinguish certain hues. If yin sees green, yang sees blue-green. Emily isn't sure she can write in blue-green, but she's trying. The only scary thing about the story so far is how contrived it is.

The tall blonde giggles again. She's at the center of the bar and still hasn't given up on charming the bartender into pouring her free drinks. Emily's sitting to the left of the blonde at the edge of the bar's leftmost corner lamenting her inability to ogle. All the good monsters have been taken.

The writer is staring at her page, not moving her pen at all, reflecting on the stagnant xenophobia that beset horror from the '90s and '00s… She has to say "excuse me?" when the bartender asks her about a third bourbon and ginger.

Another drink might grease the wheels. Another drink and she'd like the stones to look the blonde over head to toe. But alcohol presents a dilemma. Once she's good and sauced, the words won't come to her as easily. In the "pro" column, she won't second-guess the words that do. Which is slower: a clean mind prone to doubt, or an unrepentant mind slogged by neurotoxins?

The third double comes as Emily's female character stops talking because the author stops writing because the dialogue is stilted. No one says, "But I thought you wanted this, Andrew. What about all those talks we had in the beginning of things, before we got too intimate? So bored?"

Emily admits she's consumed too many poorly-translated French novels. Feeling *les incompétents*, she uses the first sip of her latest drink as a cover for scoping out the blonde, who's standing at the center of the bar still like she doesn't know what the stools are for. She's also staring back. Feeling her eyes connect with the stranger's eyes, Emily spits the syrupy-sharp out of her mouth and into the cup.

The tattoo is a purple-black dragon, the work of a preoccupied artist. The dragon's asymmetrical expression's a cross between embarrassment and sleep deprivation. Emily imagines a tattoo artist whose lover left for good the night before, or whose beloved mother took a fatal spill down the basement steps. The artist should have stayed at home that day, but better a young woman's chest tattoo than the coronation of a biker's Prince Albert. A troubled mind leads to troubled lines.

The dragon doesn't work, but it's redeemed by its canvas. She's left the house in a slim-fitting black corset top and black slacks. She'd look ridiculous if she wasn't gorgeous. *You'll believe a man can fly.*

She's definitely looking the writer in the eye. The bartender's behind the bar pretending to stock glasses to avoid more giggling and the only other patrons, two world-weary bearded men in stained overalls, are seated at a booth on the opposite side. There are no competing narratives.

Emily sips what she spat. She's never seen another woman her age at the bar alone on a midday weekday.

To allay her embarrassment she looks down at the page. Nothing's changed. Helen has no idea what to say to Andrew. Emily doesn't know beans about what heterosexuals sound like arguing at four in the morning. The majority of Andrew's quotation marks hem in key words and stretches of ink lines Emily traced along the line's rule. She could just leave the gaps between the little marks empty, but she'd feel worse about it that way.

Then she has to shut her notebook and look up: the stranger dressed like a character from a Brom painting assumes the stool beside hers and immediately leans in. She opens with, "Hi there."

Emily's response is, "Hey." She's absolutely terrified. The gay vibe she's getting is reassuring, but it's what terrifies her most of all.

The face above the dragon's, by far the prettier of the two, pouts. "This place is boring." The infantile cutesy voice should be a red flag. Babytalking strangers is a leading sign of Crazy.

The dragon's face, face to face with her now, is indeed lopsided. One eye's bigger and rounder than the other. She's speaking babytalk and flaunting a bad tattoo, but *there's that vibe,* and *besides*, crazy is an adjective that only ever gets applied to beautiful people in hindsight. *Nunc stans*, the blonde is a knockout.

"The students don't start crawling in until five or six." Emily congratulates herself on her response to the boredom comment. It conceals her excitement and makes her seem informative. She's off to a good start.

The blonde repurposes her pout into a sneer. "This is the first time I've set foot in a bar before nine."

The writer interprets the rude comment as her own mistake—around hot girls, she tends to confuse herself for a mirror. She extends her hand suddenly, desperately, but holds it low in case the gesture is all wrong and she has to pass it off as a miscommunication. *What? I wasn't trying to shake your hand. That's stupid. Who shakes hands in a bar? I had an itch.*

The gesture pans out. The blonde's palm is warm and dry, so much so that Emily's hands must be clammy for her to feel the difference. "I'm Emily," she says.

"Michelle," the long, warm, firm, reassuring fingers introduce themselves. "I hate it, it's so old-fashioned. I used to go by Mia, but yesterday morning I decided to reinvent myself as 'X.'"

It's a funny joke. Emily would laugh except, while she's socially aloof, she has an uncanny knack for knowing when not to laugh. She feels it out: "Is it catching on?"

"Ummm. I mean, sort of. My roommate thinks it's stupid, but she's a crazy cat lady in the making, I don't care what she thinks. The boys on the hall really like it."

Boys on the hall. Dorms. Boys. Fuck. "I bet they do…"

Kevin's cute, but he has 'I don't do condoms, they're too tight' written all over him. I've already dated a Kevin, he was like that too." X continues to disappoint. Emily looks longingly at her notebook. Andrew could use a hobby.

But X drops her hand on Emily's knee and asks, "You as bored with this hole as I am?"

Dizzy from the shock, she hears herself say, "No. Well, I'm flattered." But Emily's familiar with bad dialogue, and recognizes *I'm flattered* is a phrase reserved for formula rejections. She attempts to emend herself, saying, "I'm very flattered!" X moves to draw her hand away; Emily covers it with her own before it can abandon her knee. "As in, I *enjoy* it. The good flattered. I'm surprised. You just mentioned guys, so I thought…"

"Oh, that's my bad. I'm bi." She removes her hand anyway. Emily's hand spreads its fingers in protest, like a thespian flailing his arms, begging his lover not to leave him.

Emily announces she's gay, but in a whisper, like she hasn't been out since high school, like no one knows or could possibly arrive at the conclusion judging from her spiked riot-red hair and the Hélène Cixous quotes she's drawn on her tee with fabric markers.

X curls her finger around a lock of hair and nods. "I tried gay in high school, but this goth kid Andrew I dated made me realize I could never boys up." She laughs at herself, but adds, "At the same time, I feel more at home with another woman. It's more relaxed. And *way* kinkier." Though a cheap ploy, the hint at the end puts Emily at odds with her common sense.

The characters in her story, Helen and Jean (formerly Andrew), are forced to decide their future in a four a.m. conversation after Helen witnesses Jean two-timing her in a nightmare. Helen kicks Jean—no, Marcus—awake. She doesn't tell him about the nightmare; she's embarrassed.

She complains about a lack of intimacy. She complains about a lot of things. Marcus has no context for Helen's outburst, and concludes the girl he's been sleeping with for four weeks is bonkers. He's still learning who she is, and he's learning her as someone who kicks people awake to make them feel bad about themselves.

Jean feels wronged and emasculated. He gives Helen an earful about how lucky she is he doesn't kick her out of his apartment and make her walk home. He calls her crazy in the middle of page three. Page three isn't over yet.

It's a story about the inherent loneliness of billions of Sarterian hells. It's about being young, being naïve, and being of two different sexes on top of everything else. Emily wants the conversation to leverage a sense of terror stemming from the universal fear of isolation. She wants the dialogue to sound genuine without betraying her "existential/existentialist horror" leitmotif.

She isn't having much luck meeting her goals with the story, and Helen and Marcus's dialogue is coming out appallingly bad so far, but nothing she's written for them approaches the inanity of the statement, *It's more relaxed. And* way *kinkier.*

Before Emily can talk herself down from her stupid lust, X asks what she's drinking. She asks seductively, but seductively like a girl in her early twenties who still lives on a residence hall. Any idiot could see through it, but what genius hasn't lobotomized herself for love? Name one.

"Bourbon ginger." She wants to know if the dragon has a tail.

"Oh," X says, and X rears her sad face again, her reason being that "Bourbon's an old man's drink." She asks Emily if she's ever tried a vodka cranberry.

"Yes."

"Did you like it?"

"I guess."

"You guess? Emily! Bourbon is what old men drink when they get home from their boring office jobs. You're a hot chick, you should be drinking vodka crans. You'd be delicious holding a Lemon Drop too..."

Emily changes the subject. She asks X why she's in a bar before nine.

"I ditched my econ class. The professor is such a bitch. I missed one quiz! Did she want me to come to class hung over, interrupting her dumb lecture with my dry-heaving? I told her I'd make it up today, but she's only offering me half credit, so I'm ditching that too. I don't suffer fools."

"Ah."

If the other woman Helen dreamt about manifests at the end, the story would read more like a horror story. She'd have her ending. The other woman could step out of the closet, possibly covered in blood. Helen's and Marcus's bickering could lure the reader into a false sense of what the story is about, and the climax could come as a complete shock.

"I missed a couple classes at the beginning of the semester. She's pretending she's mad about my attendance, but if you ask me it's because she's in her thirties and she's starting to feel old. All she talks about is her stupid baby…"

But the buildup would have to anticipate the climax without tipping the reader off. For unity's sake. Subtlety is what distinguishes great writers from their critics.

"I hate it here. Do you want to come back to my room?"

Marcus, Helen, and the apparition vanish. "Excuse me?"

"My stepdad just bought me a surround system. We could space out on the futon. See where it goes."

"You want me to come back to your dorm room?"

"I have a huge music collection. My last ex pirated like every indie CD ever recorded. He was really into that stuff."

"So you have an akashic music library," Emily chuckles.

"What are you talking about? You sound like an old man again! Stop ruining this. You're hot. *Act hot.*"

Having the woman in Helen's nightmare walk out creates a problem of *why*. If the question isn't answered, the story will have to function in such a way that the reader doesn't expect an explanation. In other words, she'll have to revise what she already has.

"I want to make out with you." Not from X, but from Emily. The admission *accidentally* leaks from her subconscious to divert her from the threat of revision.

"Easy! I didn't think you had it in you." X tries to come off as impressed, but she's accustomed to being the bold one.

X doesn't like being upstaged. She bites her lower lip like a tired billboard model blinded by the flash of a freelancer's hot shoe flash. Her nipples have been hard for over an hour, the gooseflesh will be removed digitally, she has a three-year old at home and an addiction to menthol cigarettes that she uses to offset her cravings for food. "We can go back to my room and fool around on my couch," she teases.

Emily hasn't been with a woman in nine months. You have to take what you can get. You're only young once. There's nothing wrong with having a little fun. It doesn't have to go *all the way*. It should go *all the way*. Is the skin raised? Can the dragon fly? Kathy Acker would tell her to go for it.

Before she says yes, Emily remembers her undergraduate stereotypes. She asks, "Will your roommate be there?"

X's hotline eyes falter. "I don't know her class schedule on Thursdays. All she does is watch movies on her computer anyway."

Emily listens as her heart breaks. But that's not it. Choice parts of her are fuming, but the heart isn't involved. The heart simply supplies her choice parts with blood.

"I'm, actually, I can't," she lies. "I'm working on this story. I need to finish," she lies.

"For class?"

"No. It's a story I want to write."

X humphs. "You're only a writer if you've been published. Have you been published?"

"In the literary magazine."

"Doesn't count. My roommate had a poem in last year about her parents' divorce. It was called, 'The Pain of My Parents Divorcing.'"

Emily remembers. Winces. "I think a writer is a type of person. Writing isn't about market value."

"What's it about then?"

Emily gulps. "Writing?"

"No, your story." X pounces on the notebook and drags it toward her with her long fingers before Emily can stop her. She begins reading.

"It's not done!"

"So?" Then, as tedium instantly sets in, "What's it about?"

Emily means to wrench the notebook away but sees the bartender watching. She imagines being kicked out. She couldn't bear that ending. Not while the sun's still up. Charles Bukowski already claimed that idea.

The writer doesn't know how to explain the things she does. But she's incomplete and in enemy hands. She feels obligated to defend herself. She searches her store of words, but she's had too much to drink. "It's supposed to be about, I'm not good at explaining, it's just."

Emily's a mouth of asbestos. Rats squirm under her skin. The pores on her brow choke on their own grease and continue to spit out more, more, more in rapport with her palms and back.

Marcus kicks Helen out on the street. She leaves crying. He jerks off thinking about the strange woman he was dreaming of before Helen kicked him awake.

X is sick of reading. "I have no idea what's happening," she whines.

The girl of Helen's dreams steps out of the closet, her nightgown soaked in menstrual blood, and fingerbangs Helen. Marcus watches and tries to pleasure himself but can't. The blood won't follow him there. The heart won't have any part of it.

Emily says, "This is the worst thing in the world." She locks eyes with the bartender. He turns away aggravated. *We define out of despair.* Paraphrasing an important French philosopher. Looking around, not finding his name among the detritus.

"What? Blowing your chance to come home with me?"

Don't say it out loud. It repeats the death. She can't remember the rest. It's not even plagiarism. "What if the cup's empty?"

Her gums draw together dry from a lack of words. The click's louder than anything she's ever written.

Losers

We lose when I put another dollar
in the slot machine and make it sing.

We lose as you tap the lucky meerkat on the screen,
you read its mechanical mind.

We might win a dollar or two.

We lose our worry when the waitress
waltzes by, short skirt, short shirt, guilt

and gold. "Whiskey sour—the girl, Hennessey
for my enemies, and a green

Heineken for me." I tip her

a dollar. "Hey brother, holler at me
when you need another." Then

we lose the walls built between you and me
when the dark drinks hit our heads and the

shadows start to swim and sink

along the whispering windowless walls.
We lose sight of the time passing as

our senses fail in this infinite

night among the whispering of windowless

walls and I lose my paycheck to the

house when the beer makes me too brave and then
you lose your mind yelling when

I slide in my last dollar, another
dollar. Another one hundred pulls

before the machine starts to flash

"Losers."

Nous Sommes

"We are in the most indescribable mess."

Mrs Bellucci noticed the word "we." Professor Henry had, up until now, not been noted for extending even the most basic courtesies to the other members of his dwindling faculty, so this new found collegiality was unpersuasive. The leaves were falling even as they spoke, exposing the bones of branches through a few clumps of dishevelled grey-brown foliage. A first year with crinkled clothing straight from the tumble-drier scurried past them. Mrs Bellucci hadn't wanted to comment, had hoped to impress with a show of indifference, which was all that this rude, self-obsessed man with whom she had worked alongside for twenty-five years deserved. Then she heard herself saying: "So it's as bad as we feared." How had she let that pronoun "we", with its alluring complicity, slip out.

"Oh worse, much worse. I doubt whether I shall ever be allowed to teach a complete sentence of German again. Not now that we're amalgamating with Business Studies."

How long was it since the Department of Italian and Renaissance Studies had been swallowed up by the School of Modern Languages and this man had emerged as Dean of all he surveyed? Fifteen years at least. And during all that time he had never once addressed her by her Christian name. Probably didn't even know what it was. At meetings he looked out of the window when she spoke, and when it was impossible to avoid referring to some point that she'd made, usually about the eccentricities of the timetable, he always spoke of her as Mrs Bellucci, with a pronounced emphasis on the first two syllables, which suggested his astonishment that anyone without a doctorate from one of the three universities of which he approved could find it in themselves to express an opinion in his presence. "So it's absolutely definite then?"

"Didn't you see the Vice-Chancellor's letter? His eyes were slipping around behind his glasses. The frames were heavy and black and the thicker of the two lenses magnified a swirl of iris, cornea and pupil that seemed to be moving closer without actually looking at her. Though they had passed each other in the corridor day after day, waited in line in front of a succession of ever more technologically sophisticated coffee machines, collected photocopies of reading lists and notes from the same office, peered into neighbouring pigeon holes for memos and overdue essays, this was the first time they had stood so close and exchanged more than a sentence or two.

"I've probably got it somewhere. I'm afraid I'm not always very good at opening mail that doesn't look interesting." Why was it that she had allowed herself to get into the habit of giving her pigeon hole no more than the briefest of inspections? Sometimes she went for weeks without clearing it out properly, exposing the geological strata of unwanted correspondence.

"He did send a summary by email, as well," Professor Henry added reproachfully. She remembered that ensuring that communications between the different outposts of his empire ran smoothly was part of his remit.

"Well, how many jobs are we likely to lose? "

"He wasn't specific, but I'd say at least five. Possibly more."

It would probably mean the end of Italian altogether. Marinetti and she were the only two left. In a way one had to admit that it made sense. A kind of final tidying up. And anyway how long was it since they had done any good work? They'd had no doctoral candidates for ages, and all their students were reading for joint honours degrees, usually combining Italian with French. They'd tried to crank out the occasional article on predictable subjects to look as if they were maintaining their research. But now it seemed that no one was to be allowed to study a foreign language without combining it with estate agency, international business law or hotel management. There would be no more Leopardi, Montale, let alone Ariosto and Dante. And for that matter no more Villon, Racine, Moliere, Stendhal, Flaubert, Balzac, Proust and Camus, either. Just a few lucid little phrases about golf courses and exchange rates.

"Of course, it's barbarism," he continued, "undiluted barbarism. I've tried to speak out but it's quite impossible to get through to them. Naturally they don't think of themselves as vandals. Just realists responding to the demands of the market and government directives."

He had turned away from her, and seemed to be addressing distant figures moving purposefully about the campus, their heads bowed against the wind, one of them carrying a briefcase. She'd heard that he had married again and produced a second family late in life. There were two small boys at a private school and fees to be paid. No doubt taking early retirement was not an attractive option. Could he cling on, with Heine and Goethe and even Grass consigned in their crates to second-hand bookshops, themselves destined, no doubt, to close in year's time. How important was it to order cups of tea in German? She'd heard it bruited about that the Vice Chancellor favoured the newly opened departments teaching Mandarin and Japanese. And Islamic Studies was known to be well worth supporting: of obvious relevance to the modern world and capable of attracting outside funding in its own right; hiring an extra scholar or two would appease local opinion, and could even, in time, be a force for moderation, a counterweight to rogue madrassas flourishing in the mildewed Victorian terraces of Balsall Heath. Professor Henry seemed to have forgotten her presence. He was gazing at the red brick buildings, the steps leading up to library, now free from the students who had thronged there all summer. Perhaps he was thinking that, whether he liked it or not, this could be his last year.

Once she'd reached her room, she consulted the timetable: she was early again, not due to teach for another hour. A pile of unmarked essays sat brazenly on one of the chairs in front of her desk. As she stepped over the proofs of an article that she had written for a learned journal and circumnavigated an unsteady tower of reference books, she wondered why her home was so much tidier than her place of work. It was partly, of course, because home was so much larger, but also that now there was no one cook for, no child to put to bed and read to, there was so much more time to clean, to polish - to ensure that each treasured object, the remains of life that had once been happy, was returned to gleam in its rightful spot.

At least today her desk was not so conspicuous in its disorder. An attempt had been made to organise some documents neatly, so that that they lay flush against the sides of the in-tray. Areas of uncovered wood were visible, the telephone was not at its customary haphazard angle on top of the dictionary. No doubt this comparative tidiness was due to the fact that half the things that had once been on the desk were now on the floor. As she looked at the shelves opposite, she realised that with just a little energy it would be possible to create sufficient space to accommodate some of the volumes that now lay under her desk, on the window sill, and spread over three tables, including the one where students had once placed cups of coffee and used ashtrays, a time when the air had been wreathed with smoked and discussion.

She opened her lap top and accessed her documents. She'd been writing an article on someone, months ago. A poet whose name at first eluded her so that she was forced to begin searching through her files from the top. Then she remembered: Andrea Zanzotti. Not one of the easiest of writers. She was not sure that she altogether liked his work or even understood parts of it. But she'd been told at a conference that he was someone who ought to be written about. She read through her opening paragraphs and recalled exactly why she had reached an impasse. Then as she leaned forward to reposition her cushion so that it would protect the small of her back, her eyes met those of her son, staring back , darkly joyful, from the photograph that had been on her desk - for how long? Sixteen years, she thought, quickening with grief, sixteen years.

They'd been on holiday in Guernsey. At a small hotel on the coast that she'd known since her childhood. Although there'd been days of tattered, hurrying sunlight, the sharp winds had left them shivering on the beach. She'd taken them into Peter Port to buy the crew-necked blue jumpers of the kind the fishermen wore. She still had a photograph. Her husband, handsome in the slightly petulant of manner of some Italian men, his black hair worn just too long for him to be a businessman and too well cut for him to be a student. An art historian and rising young university lecturer on holiday in a too chilly place, one hand thrust deep into a pocket, his left arm draped protectively over the shoulders of his young son. Eleven years old. Eternally eleven years. The same boy who looked out of the studio portrait on her desk. An indelibly beautiful boy with slightly wavy brown hair and the perfect, symmetrical features of some young Florentine nobleman, his eyes huge and dark and shining, rich with possibilities, as if seeing far into a future that was not to be there. But it was his smile that somehow still set the tears stinging. It had no Renaissance gravity; it was the guilelessly contemporary smile of a loved child, exposing such perfect teeth. How long had it been after that photograph had been taken. A month at the most. Then eleven years old for ever.

There was a knock at the door and a student entered with an essay that he handed to her with an air of relief. He was still wearing a T-shirt - as if he could bring summer back. As he turned to make his way out, she reflected that he was probably not much older that she had been at her first meeting with Giovanni. It was her last year at Girton, reading Italian; he was on some sort of post-doctoral fellowship and a member of Peterhouse. They'd been introduced by her tutor at a small party to welcome a visiting Italian poet. She'd had the baby not long after graduating and they'd spent an uncomfortable year in a tiny flat above a cheap clothes shop not far from the station. Then they'd both landed teaching jobs at the same university in the Midlands. "We are so lucky," she had heard herself say, one day when she sat alone right at the front on the top deck of the bus, watching the trees pass vividly green about her; "so lucky." With two salaries they'd been able to afford the rent on a small red-bricked house in Harborne. It had a garden with one mature tree, a lawn with a birdbath right in the centre, where Marco watched the sparrows splash and chatter and sing. And people were easier, less concerned about where they had come from or were going to. She felt her cold Cambridge wit begin to thaw. There were conferences in Milan, Padua and Bologna. On a trip to Rome, Marco had been shown off to his grandparents, who were so well-dressed and dignified, and with such fine paintings in an apartment that had once been owned by a prince. "We are so lucky," she told Giovanni one night when eating on pavement outside a café alive with music, silver and elegantly circling waiters. He had looked down and smiled. Not a smile that his son would inherit, even briefly, but one that was just grateful for the moment, yet could not forget the thousand feuds and promises that had made his blood.

The door opened slightly and Marinetti peered in over his glasses before entering. He was a small, youngish man with surprisingly fair hair and skin for an Italian. He was more interested in film than literature, though at present he was writing something on Sciascia.

"How's Zanzotti?"

Mrs Bellucci looked at the colours swirling in blackness on her lap top. "I'm afraid he's going very slowly, even for an Italian."

Marinetti laughed but looked worried. Unless they both maintained their publishing record there was probably no future for either of them. She'd heard that the students liked him. Certainly his courses were better subscribed to than hers, although that could have been because they were so much less demanding.

"I'm not sure that it wouldn't be a good idea to shelve this and try something else," she said, beginning to log off.

He moved a little closer and peered at her with some concern, the concern of someone who was both "we" and operating in the present tense. "I thought you'd written five thousand words. I'd stick to it for a little longer if I were you. A friend of mine's at Perugia. I've a feeling he knows something about Zanzotti. I'll give you the email address."

It had not been an ideal holiday for Giovanni. He found the food at the hotel tasteless and the other guests dull. After a few days his face looked thinner and his once lustrous hair coarsened, it was as if were being salted by the unforgiving winds. And once, when she'd agreed to look after Marco for the morning, he'd been defeated at golf by a man who only had one arm. Though he must have thought that the British had strange ideas about what constituted an agreeable use of their leisure time, he hadn't complained. He'd helped Marco inspect rock pools and build fortresses in the sand. There had been one good day, although strangely the only one when it had rained hard. All the other holidaymakers had crowded into the lounge and were playing cards or reading the newspapers. They'd decided to take a run in the car and somehow it had been exhilarating. Tearing down the empty roads, driving fast through the little lakes that had started to collect on the roads. Giovanni explained to Marco that many of the islanders also spoke French. Marco had just started the language and started to recite the present tense of *etre,* and when he reached *nous sommes* he suddenly shouted, "We are going to have such a wonderful holiday, we are, we are! And this is an island so I'm going to find treasure and a parrot." They all started to laugh, wondrously together. Then Marco said "What's the Italian for 'we are?'" and Giovanni told him.

They went for a swim on only one occasion, just days before they were due to fly back. All three of them had spent an hour constructing an enormous sandcastle complete with a keep, a curtain wall and even some crenellations. Marco had insisted on digging out a dungeon for imaginary prisoners and a strong room in which to hide treasure. It was just very slightly warmer than usual, and, after some resistance from Giovanni, they decided that it would be cowardly return home without having taken even one dip in the sea. Leaving Marco and Giovanni to change delicately behind the screen that they erected to shield them from the wind, she walked further along the beach. A pale sun emerged from behind some thin torn clouds. A small ship was sailing towards a white horizon. When she emerged from the sand dunes, she saw that Giovanni and Marco were already making their way down the sea: high-stepping over rocks and seaweed and then speeding up as they reached the glistening sands.

"Yes, yes," she replied. "that would be helpful." Marinetti looked puzzled, as if he could not understand why she had taken so long to answer. "Thank you."

Giovanni hurdled a few small waves before diving straight through a breaker, disappearing for an instant as the green-grey, steel-flecked wall turned to foam. Then seconds after, there he was - bobbing in the trough. For a moment, she watched Marco shuffle gingerly in, his arms spread outwards like a seabird balancing on air, until suddenly he was up to his waist in water. Then he seemed to sit down, as if he were trying to perch on the edge of a sofa. It was colder than she could have imagined was possible in summer, and she began a vigorous crawl diagonally across the bay. When she looked up, there was no sign of Marco. Treading water, she turned around and around. A voice somewhere inside her was fighting an urge to scream. And then he was there. Spluttering about fifteen yards away from her, yelling something about diving for treasure.

Five minutes later they were back on the beach. Giovanni, pale beneath his tan, changed quickly and said he was going back to the hotel. As she towelled Marco vigorously, his teeth chattered and he began to shiver, but in spite of this he seemed oblivious to his physical discomfort. His eyes were shining and he was talking about treasure, which had been left by pirates. He knew exactly where it was, but he hadn't been able to reach it. Once he was dry and had a shirt on, she'd made her back to the dune only to find that her clothes had gone. She walked round it several times, but nothing was there apart from sand through which a few ragged green plants poked. Maybe Giovanni had collected her belongings and taken them straight back to the hotel. But he had walked off in the opposite direction to dune. Then it occurred to her that the wind had blown sand across her clothes. She searched around for anything that might to be the shape of a collar, a buckle or the edge of her towel. She was just about to start digging when she saw another dune, further off. She ran over quickly and there were her clothes, exactly as she had left them.

As she walked back, she saw that the tide was coming in fast, eating the beach away until it was little more than a narrow strip between the sea and the rocks. The sun was gone and a strange grey light charged the landscape with an ambiguous luminosity. There wasn't a single bird in the sky. A wave touched her feet and withdrew, sketching silver over the pebbles. Then she realised the sandcastle had vanished. She felt a quick stab of unfamiliarity and turned round to see if she had walked back the wrong way, but there were the dunes, the larger of the two shaped like a burial mound. Desperately she began to run in the direction of higher ground when she saw the wind-break and carrier bag, still safe under nook in the rock face. She told herself that Marco was already on his way back but there was no sign of him on the path that led to the hotel. By the time that she reached wind-break and looked behind she already knew that he would not there. His clothes were lying on top of his towel, including the shirt that she'd helped him to put on. There was no one on the beach as far as the eye could see. The ship had disappeared over the horizon.

She hadn't noticed Marinetti leave and now there was another knock on the door.

Three sharp, authoritative raps. Not, she thought, a student.

"Come in." She sounded hoarse.

Professor Henry opened the door. His eyes looked huge and startled, as if he were afraid of the mess. After a brief deliberation he stepped forward very slightly, so that his front foot was almost touching a document wallet that lay near the start of the direct root between the door and the desk. She could just see that on one corner of the wallet there was part of a dry footprint, possibly made by one of her students. Professor Henry had left the door slightly open.

"Sorry to interrupt," There was the beginning of a bark in his voice.

He looked around the room again, as if he suspected there might a student or two hiding under the furniture. And then he coughed. "I just thought I'd let you have a look at this." He was holding an A4 manila envelope. Mrs Bellucci saw that his green tweed jacket was not large enough for him and his left trouser leg had two creases. This was the first time he had ever been in her room. "Something in the nature of a plan of action," he said. "We are nothing if we don't stand together on this one. Take a good look at it. Comments in pencil, please. Then put it back in its envelope and give it to my secretary." He took two long strides forward, narrowly missing her article on Montale, before leaning forward as if he were trying to stretch across a chasm. She stood up and was just able to take the envelope from him.

They buried Marco on the island. Her mother came out, but her father had been too ill to make the journey. No one came from Italy, so there had been just three people who had known him on the day they stood in the cemetery under another dry grey day that always threatened rain. And always the wind, blowing immortally.

The start of the new academic year had saved them for a time, driven them out of the too quiet house. But once, just a few days after they'd returned, she'd laid up breakfast for three people, and Giovanni had found her sobbing in the kitchen. As soon as the students were back, and they had their different timetables, they took meals separately, were always careful to wash up afterwards - as though to have eaten at all was some kind of betrayal. At Easter, Giovanni had gone to Rome - alone. He was away for a week. A short visit to see his parents, he said. But when he came back he was even more withdrawn and they started to sleep in separate rooms. A full year passed before he told her. He'd accepted a new job in Italy. His parents were growing old and he needed to be nearer to them. And, oh yes, there was somebody else. It wasn't serious at the moment, but might become so one day.

And now her students were in front of her. The one with the beard had moved a pile of books off a chair and was looking around for somewhere to put them. She hated hearing herself having to teach: the cadences of her old Cambridge tutor were in her voice: a practiced distance, a cold, precise wit. In autumn, it was a Cambridge fog that hovered outside the window, looking at the way she sat back in her chair, how she stared indifferently at the ceiling, whilst turning a long thin pencil in her long thin fingers.

At last, when they had finally settled, had taken out books and essays and notepads, rummaged through pockets for missing biros, taken off jackets and then put them on again, she began.

"We are, as I think I may have promised last time we met …."

We are, we are … this was all she ever wanted to say again, if only she could mean it, feel it, not misuse it: *nous sommes*, we are. How to be together and not alone, in any language.

Grace

What it is:
Charlemagne's dog
Can't stop licking
Blood away from the day –
Stands ready – toothy –
Carried by historical sense
To stay bottom-rusted to greatness
But always upward glancing
Singing in dog to Christ
Who feigns interest.
What it is:
Dying from remaining
A holy K-9 covenant
watching the last shock
When veins pop and blood
Like oil bubbles
On the marble surface,
Red splattered Lame';
And finally
A joining of verse to frailty
The body humbly mastered
Clean of tomorrow.

Snapshots

There were posers all around. That's the word he would use as he dismissed them. With skinny pants and scarves artfully tied about their necks, they peered at their iMacs and sipped half caf, double soy lattes. It was the sort of place they used to joke about going into just to ruin the hip factor. She stirred her coffee again and waited. She might have made a tactical error. With his disdain for such people, he probably would not have a problem making a public scene here. She arranged the empty sugar packets on the table to make a little picture frame that highlighted a swirl of brushed steel.

It reminded her of a coffee place they had found in central Oregon. The industrial chic décor was highlighted by the Christian Patterson prints on the walls; a black and white picture of a white walled tire here, a shot of a multi-colored fluorescent light there. The tables rocked a bit on the uneven, reclaimed wood floor. That place hadn't done quite enough demographic research. Besides them, the only other customers were two men wearing dirty Carhartt pants and hooded sweatshirts. The barista, with his ironic mustache, did not hide his disgust when they ordered plain black coffees. They had taken pictures of each other in front of all the art on the walls while the two guys watched them. She stirred her coffee again.

On that same trip through Oregon, their car had broken down on an empty two lane highway in southern Utah. In an hour, not one car passed, and the auto club said it would be at least three hours before a tow truck would arrive. He had found a box of pastel chalks in the trunk and first they played hopscotch in the middle of the road. Then they drew pictures of bunnies and cats and saguaro cactus and city skylines. The county sheriff who finally came by threatened to cite them for defacing public property. Their Christmas card that year was a photo of him arguing with the sheriff; both of them standing in a sea of Easter colors.

A woman entered pushing an Uppa Baby stroller. She had black, thick framed glasses and wore yoga pants and knee high black leather riding boots. Her child reached out a chubby hand and knocked over a display of coffee beans. It was tough to be hip with a toddler. He was good with children. He built forts with his nephews and had stuffed animal tea parties with her niece. He was the cool uncle and, when they babysat, always ensured that the kids returned home riding raging sugar highs. Once, when his nephew was two, he took a picture of little Ethan sleeping with a bottle of scotch, a cigar, and an old issue of Playboy. He hid the picture in Ethan's little backpack to be found later by his mother.

She sipped her coffee and looked at her sugar framed metal swirl. The design was etched permanently into the surface. Her phone vibrated. It was a text from her sister.

"Well?" she asked.

"He's not here yet," she thumbed back.

"Call me after!"

He hated texting. They had been at a restaurant in Newport once, dining outdoors over the water. A couple at a table next to them never said a word to one another. They never even looked up from their smart phones. He had reached over, taken the woman's phone and tossed it into the bay.

"Have a conversation," he said. She sat looking on while profanities were exchanged. He was arrested, booked complete with mug shots, and released.

She looked at the time on her phone and rose to get another coffee. There was the time he was late for her sister's wedding. It was an outdoor garden affair so all the guests could see when he got out of the cab still dressed in the clothes he had worn to the bachelor party the night before. He had waved, bowed deeply, told the minister to carry on, and everyone except her sister and her father had laughed. He managed to be in just about every wedding picture.

Two teenaged girls in front of her were having difficulty deciding between the iced caramel latte or the mocha cappuccino. There had been lovely flowers at her sister's wedding. All manner and color of roses were deeply in bloom, infusing the air, and she had thought she might like to have her own wedding there. The girls settled on the cappuccinos and moved on to debating biscotti. After seeing his apartment for the first time, she had brought him a plant to brighten it up. It was a begonia she had grown from a cutting. He promptly killed it. She gave him a fern, a jade plant and then a spider plant. They all died, not from neglect, but from overwatering. She finally gave him a bamboo that he could not love to death. It grew and grew, and he posted a pic of it for his blog cover.

"Small black coffee," she said.

"One small old school," the cashier called back to the barista. Plain coffee had become an anachronism. It seemed to her that things changed when she wasn't looking.

She sat again and traced the swirls on the metal with her fingertip. She added sugar packets to her table top picture frame to make it more substantial. The extra heft highlighted the design even more. He passed by the window in front of her, and the bell on the door clanged.

She swept the sugar packets aside, and the brushed swirl disappeared into the rest of the design. It was time.

Banksville

"Banksville," that's what it was, hurtling southbound on the Merritt. Construction confuses him, though, signs covered, ramps razed and barricaded. They'd always turned here, at the New York State line. His calloused old hands tighten on the wheel. "This is it," he promises, "we're going the right way."

The road he wants appears, curving into the hills north of the highway. But he gets distracted and suddenly, he's in New York. His heart pounds; this is what the doctor warned him about. He panics: maybe it's been too long. Everything seems that way lately, that's why he likes to tell old, familiar stories.

But she's with him, and he has to take care of her. Honey, he thinks, am I all you've got? Is this it for you? Then, it has to be enough.

"I'll reverse direction." But he misses all the exits, they come too soon. He catches his breath, picks one, and plunges into a gulley between cones. He veers through the gap like riding a bronco, and he's back on the highway.

Up ahead, he sees the ramp again and shoots off onto a fringe of asphalt. They glide, slowing, letting the car nose its way along skinny backroads canopied with trees. The leaves turn sunlight to lace, greening the air, slanting shadows he can drive into as if they were deep pools.

His body is worn out, they say he needs an operation. But here, the air is sweet with cut grass. He can travel at his own pace and take his daughter, who, grown, still can't seem to find her own way.

Swinging the car around like the needle of a compass, he says, "My grandfather used to take me to the fair at Banksville. It's an old country town. I got my first fishing rod there. We used to go fishing together. It was just a field where trucks used to pull up, selling tools, household things, and bushels of produce. You could make deals. You could bargain. They held auctions Saturday."

"Sounds great," she says, smiling at him.

"I haven't been there in forty years," he warns. "It's probably changed quite a bit. They used to advertise it on the radio."

"They'll have just what we're looking for."

He nods. Now that she's on her own again, she needs the right tools, in case she has to fix something. He has a list in his mind, starting with a garden.

"You have to buy the whole bushel. You can't pick and choose."

"Okay," she says. She tucks her hair behind her ears, ready for action.

He drives due north on backroads, until they come suddenly to the end. The road has been rerouted. There's a gate, now. A country club. Shaved lawns cover slopes on either side, pillared with spreading golf-course trees.

"I should've brought the map," she says, looking pointlessly through her purse.

"Maybe it's gone."

He tries to hide this feeling that the world has dropped away and left him hanging somewhere in space. If her brothers had lived, he might have taken them to Banksville in the meantime, and then he'd have known what was going on. He'd have kept in touch. But they didn't. They died young, in fact, so there's been no need to come here for years. Nobody to dig gardens with, or fish with, or build with. Now, her mother's gone, too.

He turns the car around and drives back down the road, toward home.

"I left the map on the counter."

"You could've brought it, like I asked."

She says nothing.

Maybe the things a man like him is good at don't matter any more. If that's so, he's ready to face it. He always faces things. But what will become of her? That thought haunts him.

They pull into the driveway and park. She gets the road atlas and spreads it out on the trunk of the car. He goes to look at it. There, at the state line, is printed the name, "Banksville."

"So, it does exist," says the man. He traces the road over and over with his broad, work-hardened finger while his daughter dials information and calls a hardware store listed for the town. Then she hangs up and faces him.

"The market's been gone for years," she says. "This guy built his store where it used to be."

The old man straightens up and rubs his sore back. He feels embarrassed, for some reason. So he climbs back into the car, his prosthetic body, his life, it seems, only moving smoothly on four wheels these days.

She leans down to the open window. "I'm sorry."

"What can you do."

"We'll plant a garden anyway. You just tell me what to do."

Trusting. Planning. As if he always could tell her things, as if he'd always be there.

"We'll dig up the whole yard," she says. "That's what the land is for, right? We'll grow tomatoes and fruit trees and beans and flowers and pumpkins."

Her father nods. What else can you do? You make promises, hoping you can keep them. Knowing you can't, but making them, anyway.

“Is that what hope is? Defeated at birth?

Then, let an old man get at it. He'll show everybody. All he needs is some swing room and one of his good days.

He puts up a hand and waves and pulls back out of the driveway in a cloud of dust. In the rearview mirror, he watches her stand for a moment, alone, her thin silhouette arched a little at the back -- so like her mother's -- encompassed in the oval of a rearview mirror. When he leaves, she'll go in the house and shut the door, which is where he usually finds her, and the yard will fall silent.

The White Mountains

The family we found, in the deep woods,
Barked in our faces, like anxious bloodhounds,
Before the older ones remembered words
From a long-dead era: "hep cats," "niftic,"
The matriarch cooing "Daddy-O" as
She toyed with the strange fabric of our shirts.
We had some trouble understanding them,
But could read all their hard years in the pelts
Hanging from the rafters of their cabin,
Their black teeth and scars, the missing eyeball
Of the father who begged us for a smoke.
The children ran on all fours and stole our
Shiny things, their mother talked to spirits
Lurking (she believed) in the stone of the
Crude hearth. We brought them the modern world, boxed
In plastic crates: sweaters, shoes, freeze-dried food,
But only then, trussed in bright synthetics,
Shorn like pets awaiting the vet's scalpel,
Did they seem like something to be pitied.

To Stop a Cockfight

They were a very famous couple. He was a world-renowned artist and drunk and she was just as well known for her extravagant and highly destructive emotional breakdowns. They would roar into a town – New York, Los Angeles, Paris – like a whirlwind. Exuding charm and sophistication and displaying a world class penchant for alcohol, drugs and histrionics, they would inevitably become embroiled in some sort of dust up with the locals that typically led to his arrest or detainment and a trip to rehab for her. It was all a lot of lovely fun and they were frightfully good at it.

"Let's go to Havana," she proposed one evening when they had become fully bored with New York and had worn out their welcome there anyway. "We can get a room by the water and have wonderful parties every night. Champagne, fresh sea food, fresh people."

"Sounds swell," he admitted, "but I'm supposed to be finishing a painting this week. We'll need that big payday."

"Can't you just get an advance?" she asked. "You're good for it. You can finish it when we get back."

"Oh, baby," he sighed.

She sidled up next to him and slipped a hand down the front of his pants.

"Ooh," he moaned.

"Please," she whispered directly into his ear. He twisted under her sensual assault. "It'll be worth your while."

"No doubt," he said huskily.

"Now, call your stupid agent or the gallery and get us some money for Cuba," she said, slowly pulling her hand back out of his slacks. "I'm going to pack."

"Right this minute?" he asked breathlessly.

"Unless you have something better in mind," she teased, holding her hand out towards him.

"You're taunting me," he said.

"You're boring me," she responded.

"Let me come help you pack," he said suggestively.

"Packing is what you like best, right baby," she played.

"Get up there," he told her, "and you'll find out."

"You get up," she laughed.

With a wild roar, he chased her up the stairs to their spacious bedroom. She was still laughing when he caught her and wrestled her onto the bed.

"You are so easy," she said.

"You've been reading the tabloids again, haven't you?" he joked.

"TMZ," she giggled. "I saw it on TMZ."

* * *

Through friends in the art community who had contacts among the Washington high muckety mucks, he had wrangled visas for the two of them on the pretense they were part of an international artist exchange. He was banking on the government not realizing the exchange was a bogus program until after the trip and they were back in the states. He was sure Cuba wouldn't care. It would look good for their open borders program and the greenbacks he was known to throw around so loosely would be icing on the international visitor cake.

They arrived at the International Terminal of José Martí Airport around 8 p.m. and, after clearing Customs with a minimum of hassle, grabbed a taxi to the Hotel Cienfuegos near Havana Bay. Havana was still plenty warm and very humid, like any tropical Caribbean city would be even though it was evening.

"Welcome to Havana," the friendly, English-speaking clerk told them when they checked in. "Mr. and Mrs. Sheridan," he added, checking their passports and then returning them with a smile.

"Where can we find a good bar with happening people?" Mr. Sheridan asked the clerk.

"Oh, Carlton," Mrs. Sheridan laughed, feigning embarrassment. "We needn't go out the moment we arrive in town."

"Au contraire, mon Zoe," Carlton told his wife. "That's exactly when we should go out." Zoe laughed gaily at her impulsive husband.

"He's such a bon vivant," Zoe explained to the clerk as if it were a medical condition that might need quarantining.

"You might try the Floridita," the helpful clerk said. "It was the favorite place of your Mr. Hemingway."

"Ah, yes," Carlton said dramatically, "good old Ernest. He knew all the right places to drink. And I, Carlton F. Sheridan, good old American artiste, shall follow in Papa's glorious steps."

"Glorious Papa killed himself with a shotgun," Zoe reminded Carlton. The clerk averted his eyes from the flamboyant couple.

"And more's the tragedy for it," Carlton said, with a wild wave of his left arm. "All the more reason to share a libation in the gray-bearded one's ex-drinking hole."

"Before we even drop our things off in the room and freshen up a bit?" Zoe wondered.

"Hardly my dear," Carlton kept up the master thespian routine. "We will retire to our temporary lodgings and prepare for the evening's entertainment. We're hardly animals, are we?"

"Thank you, young man," Zoe told the clerk, when he handed her the key to their room, Carlton already trundling towards the lobby elevator.

"A sus ordenes," the clerk said, unable to resist a lengthy appraisal of Zoe's considerable physical charms. "At your service."

Zoe gave the young man a flirty wink and followed after Carlton who was already engaged in a conversation with the elevator attendant.

* * *

"I don't see anything so special about this place," Zoe said, from her seat at the bar in the Floridita.

"Like you can't see the life-sized statue of Papa by the bar down there?" Carlton said, holding out his arm and pointing to their left.

"I'm surprised somebody didn't stuff him and set him on a stool with a daiquiri in his hand."

"Ah, yes," Zoe replied, not even looking over at the statue of Hemingway, "the world famous daiquiris in the world famous Floridita. I feel like I just got off the cruise boat. Can we get any more touristy you suppose? Where the hell is that bartender?"

The bartender was nearby and quite accommodating. He made daiquiri after daiquiri for the Sheridans even when he should have stopped. Neither of them could really handle their liquor and they tended to make scenes, even squawking and laughing over the sounds of an old trio that played wonderful local music while the wealthy gringo patrons, the Sheridans first among them, got perfectly sloshed.

Around midnight, at last tired of daiquiris, the Sheridans stumbled out of the Floridita into the moist Havana night. They managed to hawk down a taxi and were able to convey to him their desire for continued partying. The driver took them to an upscale drinkery down by the harbor where they encountered a lovely young working woman who was amenable to their off-menu desires – for agreed upon compensation. Back at the hotel, the threesome found the Sheridans' bed to be quite adequate for energetic physical activity.

"Her skin," Zoe said dreamily, caressing the young woman's inner thigh, "so brown and silky soft."

"Marcela," Carlton said, in between kisses with their new companion, "her name is Marcela."

"Yes," Zoe said, "Marcela."

Marcela writhed beneath Zoe's touch and Carlton's deep kisses. They occupied her then at both top and bottom. She moaned with pleasure. The sheets on the bed twisted beneath the voluptuaries into a labyrinth of wet, soft fabric. Finally, the threesome lay still, satiated with temporal contentment.

"What we need," Carlton proclaimed, after some quarter of an hour of rest and quiet, "is something more to drink."

The women, sleeping in each other's arms, did not hear him, so Carlton rang up the desk and ordered a bottle of whiskey and a magnum of red wine. While his wife and their consort slept, Carlton drank shot after shot of whiskey and used the red wine as a chaser. All went well until about dawn.

"Oh," Carlton belched, his stomach rumbling and rolling violently, "I feel sick."

Clambering out of bed, he caught his feet in the sheets and fell face first on the floor. Grunting, he drug himself towards the bathroom on skinned up hands and knees. On the bed, the women rolled away from each other but neither woke. Carlton kept pulling himself along and barely made it to the bathroom before unleashing a torrent of yellowish-red liquid into the commode. He hurled and hurled. When there was no more liquid left, he began to wretch, dryly, loudly. It finally woke Zoe up. She slowly wound her way off the bed and into a wobbly upright position.

"Oh," she groaned, holding her aching head.

Through bleary eyes she saw Carlton emerge from the bathroom. Thin lines of blood covered his lower lip and chin. He was slightly bent and holding his stomach. Zoe stumbled towards him.

"Baby, baby," she cried, "you're bleeding. You're bleeding out your mouth."

"Threw up," Carlton mumbled, smearing the blood on his face with the back of his hand. "Sick."

Zoe screamed and wretched herself. She fell to one knee and began to cry.

"No," Carlton said, "no, baby. Not now. Don't lose it now."

But it was too late. Zoe was in the throes of a nervous attack. She was on the floor, back arched above the damp carpet, eyes rolled back in her head. She made a sound like a low-decibel scream coming from too deep inside her to be fully released into the air. Carlton reached out for her, but was so weak from vomiting that he simply fell unconscious by her side.

* * *

Around ten-thirty that morning, with the sun shining brightly into the hotel room, Carlton woke. His throat burned like fire itself and his chest rattled with every deep breath. Crawling, stumbling out of bed he went straight for the only cure he knew – more alcohol. He found it in a nearly empty bottle of Scotch lying on the bathroom floor. He downed it with one long swig.

"What the hell," he mumbled, noting the dried blood stains on the floor through watery red eyes.

He wobbled back out to the bedroom looking for Zoe and the girl they had picked up. The girl was nowhere to be seen but Zoe lay on the carpet beside the bed in a fetal position. Carlton knelt beside her.

"Wake up, baby," he said, shaking Zoe's shoulders. "Get up."

Zoe just pulled herself into a tighter ball. She moaned lowly. Carlton looked around the room for more alcohol and something to smoke. Finding neither, he called down to the front desk for room service. They would find the items for the gentleman right away they said. They would have a bellboy bring them right away. They were happy to accommodate the lovely North American couple they said.

While he waited on his whiskey and cigarettes, Carlton surveyed the damage in the room. Nothing broken, but everything tossed around; sheets on the floor, food containers on a table and by a chair. He looked through his billfold and Zoe's purse to see if the girl had robbed them. If she had, she had not taken much. That was a good thing.

After a few minutes, he managed to muster the strength to lift Zoe and put her in bed. She stayed curled up like a baby and he pulled the sheets over her to provide some decency for when room service arrived. There were the amenities to be accounted for after all.

Zoe woke around noon, well after the whiskey and cigarettes arrived and had been paid for. Carlton still felt like hell but the whiskey dulled the pain in his throat and chest and he nursed Zoe most of the day. As soon as she was properly awake, she went into a highly agitated, nervous state. She alternately cried, laughed, cursed Carlton. With each outburst he drank more, ordering another bottle late in the afternoon, as well as another pack of smokes. There was considerable consternation between them, much leveling of charges, uncountable accusations.

But by evening, things had begun to smooth over. She was less agitated. His throat and chest hurt less. It was time to go out again. Around nine-thirty they prepared for the evening, dressing elegantly as always, yet barely looking at one another. Outside, they found the same taxista who had ferried them about the night before and told him to find a bar that Papa had not frequented.

The zinc bar in the Hotel Parador was a long straight rectangle, worthy of Hemingway but not in existence during his time in Havana. Carlton and Zoe plopped down about mid-bar and ordered scotch on the rocks – they were beginning the evening slow. After several more rounds, they grew tired of the staid atmosphere of the Parador and had their waiting taxista score a fifth of Johnny Walker Black and some "special" smoking material that they partook of while the cabbie drove aimlessly through the dark, moist Havana night. Despite the numbing effect of the alcohol and weed, Carlton's throat and chest continued to bother him and between drinks and puffs he repeatedly hacked and coughed.

"You need a medico?" the cabbie turned around briefly to ask Carlton.

"Wha…?" Zoe mumbled. She was slumped against the back seat away from Carlton.

"My throat hurts," Carlton told the cabbie. "My chest."

"Cough medicine?" the cabbie suggested.

"Percodan," Carlton told him, "for pain. Or Oxycotin."

"Shew," the cabbie whistled, "you have to see a medico for that, señor."

"A doctor?" Zoe said, perking up. "We need a doctor."

"You know one?" Carlton asked the cabbie.

"I know one," the cabbie said, looking at Carlton in the rearview mirror. "But it cost you money."

"Let's go," Carlton said. "I'm tired of hurting."

"Yeah," Zoe chipped in, quickly re-involved in the evening, "let's see a doctor."

The cabbie took them to an especially poor looking part of town and hooked the couple up with a "medico" friend of his. Carlton produced two large denomination American bills and the doctor produced a small envelope with five pills in it.

"Only five?" Carlton asked. The doctor shrugged his shoulders. Carlton laid another big bill down and received another three pills.

"A real bargain," the cabbie said.

"Ganga," the doctor said with a sneering smile.

"Fuck you," Carlton said, taking two of the pills and downing them with a big swig of alcohol. Zoe reached for the pills but Carlton only gave her one. "We can use the others later, baby."

Twenty minutes later all the pain was gone. There was no physical pain; there was no psychic pain. Carlton felt strong and magnanimous. Zoe giggled frequently and smiled into the Havana night as if she and it shared some special Zen knowledge. They were both living in the moment and the moment was fine.

"Where next, baby?" Carlton asked, smiling at Zoe.

"Not another damned old Papa bar," she laughed.

"No more Papa bars," Carlton assured her.

"Papa bar?" the cabbie wondered out loud, not looking back.

"Nor mama bars either," Carlton wise-cracked.

"You are so clever, my sweet," Zoe said.

"I don't understand," the cabbie said.

"We want to go somewhere exciting," Zoe told him. "Somewhere different. Somewhere where tourists would never go."

"You want to go maybe to a hole in the wall cantina?" the cabbie questioned.

"No, no," Carlton told him. "A place with danger, thrills. Not boring."

"Danger, not boring," the cabbie repeated.

"You know of such a place?" Zoe asked him.

"I don't know, señora," he said, shrugging his shoulders.

“I’ve got it,” Carlton declared.

“What, what, darling?” Zoe asked excitedly.

“A cockfight. Let’s go to a cockfight,” Carlton declared.

“Splendid,” Zoe cheered.

“No,” the cabbie disagreed. “No cockfight. Very dangerous for foreigners.”

“That’s exactly why we want to go,” Carlton told him.

“Exactly,” Zoe echoed.

“No, no,” the cabbie reiterated. “Not good.”

“Perfect,” Carlton contradicted. “Take us to one right now.”

He handed the cabbie a respectable American bill.

“Sí, señor,” the cabbie said, admiring the money but still shaking his head.

“Oh, how wonderful,” Zoe said wild-eyed. Carlton celebrated with a big slug of Johnny Walker.

The cabbie drove the loco Americanos out to the edge of Havana where he knew of a semi-respectable cockfighting arena – la Gallera Matanza. He hoped the not so respectable neighborhood of the arena would dissuade them from their craziness. It did not.

“Is this it?” Zoe asked, not impressed by the wooden building housing the fights. Even at night she could see paint peeling from the walls and from around a couple of small windows on the side.

“This is it,” the cabbie said. “Maybe you want to go back to a nice bar in town?”

“No way in hell,” Carlton slurred, stumbling out of the cab. “We’re going in there and see the birdies do battle.” Zoe giggled and struggled out of the cab.

“I better take you in,” the cabbie said. “It can get a little rough.”

Inside the gallera, most of the bettors – all men save a couple women standing in the shadows at the back of the arena – ignored the new arrivals except for a few whistles and catcalls aimed at Zoe as she and Carlton struggled to find a good viewing spot. The cabbie found a place behind them and tried to discreetly blend in. For his part, Carlton kept slamming down the Johnny Walker and joined in the loud cheering of the crowd as two fighting birds were brought out for the next contest.

"Look how brightly colored they are," Zoe commented. "They're beautiful."

"Very beautiful," Carlton muttered, swaying against the wood railing. He caught himself just before he would have fallen into the dirt of the arena floor. Two nearby men roughly pushed him back.

"Keep your hands off," he said drunkenly.

"Carlton," Zoe warned. "Don't start anything." Before Carlton could come up with a response to Zoe, a roar from the crowd signaled the beginning of the fight.

One man in the ring acted as judge or referee while two other men held their fighting cocks up so that the birds could see each other. The animals immediately tried to peck each other. The audience cheered again. The judge then drew a line in the sandy floor of the arena and the bird handlers placed their birds on it. The judge signaled with his right hand and the men released the birds. It was as if chaos had been instantly unleashed in the building. Betting, cheering, jostling erupted on all sides and the birds leaped and pecked at each other while trying to slice each other up with the sharp metal spurs attached to their feet.

At first, Carlton and Zoe were into the fight. The birds were agile and courageous, fighting without taking or giving quarter. Feathers flew in all directions, with an occasional spray of chicken blood mixed in. Carlton looked down and saw some of the blood on his jacket and began howling insensibly. The combat thrilled Zoe and excited her until suddenly, one of the cocks began to get the upper hand in the fight.

With a daring, athletic leap, one cock brought his spur against the neck of the other and slit a wound across its body causing blood to fly all over the arena. As the wounded cock staggered backwards, the more powerful bird spun again and sliced the tendons on the back left leg of his opponent. The injured bird reeled to one side, falling in the blood-spattered sand. It struggled back to one foot but the other dangled in the air. The crowed roared. The sight of the cut and dying cock, horrified Zoe and she began to scream.

"Stop it, stop it," she yelled at Carlton. "Stop them. It's horrible."

Dredging up energy from some long forgotten place in his psyche and body, Carlton did as Zoe bid. He tried to leap over the railing but his left leg didn't quite clear and he landed chest-first into the sandy arena. Sliding in the sand and blood, Carlton struggled to his feet just as several men stormed into the ring after him. In seconds they were all over him – hitting, pummeling, kicking, biting and gouging – trying to punish the insane foreign interloper who dared interfere with their game.

Carlton gamely but ineffectually tried to defend himself as the punches rained down on him from all directions. He was shoved and pushed back against the wood barrier of the arena. His assailants repeatedly hit him in the face and torso until he finally fell, Zoe shrieking madly as Carlton, unconscious, bounced off the floor of the arena. Several men drug him out and tossed his inert body on the dirty floor. More people kicked him while he was down. Zoe slapped at the men but they just laughed and spun her around in all directions, some of them pawing her breasts and pinching her buttocks.

Finally, the cabbie broke through the crowd and mercifully dragged Zoe and Carlton towards the front door. Carlton regained consciousness as they were reaching the door and the cabbie helped him out just behind Zoe's fleeing form. The cabbie opened the back door of his vehicle and Zoe threw herself inside. Carlton stumbled in behind her. Back at the gallera, it was all loud cheering and laughter.

"I told you we should not go there," the cabbie said as he cranked the taxi engine and roared away from the cockfight arena.

"Shut up," Zoe cried, "you're a bastard just like all these people down here."

"That's no way …," the cabbie began.

"I told you to shut up," Zoe more sobbed than yelled. "Get us back to the hotel right now."

"Sí, señora," the cabbie said with some disgust, "as you wish."

* * *

Back at the hotel, Carlton alternately threw up blood and passed out. His face was a mish-mash of cuts and bruises. After one particularly strong retching episode, he collapsed on the floor of the bathroom and Zoe thought he might have died. In a panic she called the main desk and blubberingly demanded a doctor be sent up immediately. Carlton's breathing was shallow and slow when the doctor arrived. Zoe helped lift Carlton onto the bed where the doctor examined him.

"He's going to die," Zoe said. The doctor couldn't tell if it was a question or a statement.

"He is in a bad way," he told Zoe. "Perhaps he will not die."

"What are you going to give him?" Zoe asked, watching the doctor remove a small, dark bottle from a well-used, brown leather bag. He stuck a syringe into the end of the bottle and drew out a slightly yellow but otherwise clear liquid.

"This is Vitamin B6," the doctor said, squirting a little of the liquid from the nearly full syringe to eliminate any air bubbles. "It should make your esposo much better."

"Esposo?" Zoe wondered.

"Your husband."

"Oh."

Within a quarter hour of the injection, Carlton began to stir back to life. Zoe overpaid the doctor with the promise he would return at once if needed. After getting another type of liquid into Carlton, this time plain old boring water, Zoe settled him comfortably in bed. She nervously paced the room until sure he was breathing safely. Right away, he drifted back off and when she was sure he was just sleeping and not dead, Zoe curled up under a blanket in one of the room's chairs and fell into a troubled sleep.

Late in the afternoon of the following day, with Carlton out of immediate danger but still barely mobile, Zoe had the hotel main desk order first class air tickets for New York and call a taxi to drive them to the airport.

In New York, Carlton was hospitalized for alcohol poisoning and exhaustion. Zoe left him on the third day of his treatment and flew home to Georgia where her mother lived. In a matter of days she had become so distraught that she could neither sit still nor sleep and her mother had her put in a sanitarium where she was treated for hysteria and symptoms related to a nervous breakdown.

Over the following months, Zoe's condition worsened before it improved. She had delusions where she claimed to speak directly to Jesus Christ, William the Conqueror and Mary Queen of Scots. Several rounds of therapy, including shock treatments and heavy doses of tranquilizer drugs, deadened her to the pain of life and towards autumn of the year she was finally released.

Her mother welcomed her home with the news that Carlton had died of liver failure while Zoe had been at the sanitarium. The news neither surprised her nor affected her greatly. Something seemed to have died inside her that night of the cockfight in Cuba. She just remembered Carlton lying on the hotel floor barely breathing. Whatever they had had between them died there on that floor.

Without Carlton in her life, Zoe found, to her surprise, that she could draw and paint, too, and her work found a ready audience. Her bold slashes of brazen, bright colors on canvas was Van Gogh-like some critics said and she began to make a good living with her work and became a bit of a cause cèlébre in the art world – something about the tortured, abused soul of the submerged, restrained artist.

When she had lucid, pain-free moments, however, she remembered the earlier, better times she had shared with Carlton. In the end, her only regret, in those times of clarity, was that after Cuba she had never seen him alive again. She knew that there was nothing else she could have done, else she would have died too, had she stayed with him and they had continued their path of self-destruction. They had loved one another each in their own way but her only hope of personal survival was to escape the entropic, spiral towards certain death that was Carlton F. Sheridan – and that is what she did.

Postcards

Here's what's new with me:
I've been sleeping too much.

I'm addressing this to Andromeda:
Are you still a galaxy?
If the sun takes eight minutes to touch me
everything else takes longer.
I am waiting
watching the night skies from buses & planes
when movement moors itself to a chair—
I am willing to turn Earth into just a reflection of the sun in the sky.

For Vallie,
In Italy I thought of
when we use to hide our tongues like spare keys
in each other's mouths.
For an hour I sat looking at *David* eating a sandwich with pickles.
I remember when you went through a sculpting phase in college
but refused to sculpt any nudes of me.

Dear Mom,
I've found too many homes in the last six years.
How many corners can a sphere have?
I assume dad's getting close to retiring, tell him congrats.
Remember when you told Joseph and me that
after you die you
want us to spread your ashes around The Painted Hills?
I hope to see you before then.

To Iowa,
To kill time I've taken a ship from India to Canada.
Do you ever long for the infinite view of oceans?
Or does the corn feel like an ocean?

Vallie,
I've taken a job coaching JVII soccer in Maine.
Soccer should have been a spring sport.
Do you still play volleyball? Isn't that a winter sport?
I never could understand the role of the Libero.
I'm sorry. I figured it'd be nice to start at a neutral point
like how the tether ball always starts in your hand.
I've been thinking more of our locations compared to one another:
What stars do you see?
I found I'm allergic to cilantro.
I never used to be: perhaps allergies change
like rules.

Dear the Milky Way Galaxy,
This is a petition to allow all other worlds,
stars, planets, gas formations, galaxies and dark matter
to become a full part of you. It seems silly to separate things
that are already so separated.

To Joseph,
I'm glad you're married. I bet
she makes you work harder than you planned on working.
And, since I know you won't write back, I bet
you'll have kids. You'll be a great father. Just listen
to Sonya when she tells you how to teach, she's certified.
P.S. Mom told me to spread her ashes in Eastern Oregon when she dies.
See you soon.

A story addressed to Vallie's last known address:
Just last week I went home. I hadn't been back in years.
At McDonald's I saw the same garbage can beneath the streetlight in the parking lot—
I never told anyone about that midnight.

In response to the Sun's petition to remain the center of our solar system,
When did you ever think we didn't need you to breathe?
Let's be honest for once: We want to hold you close
burn you into our bodies
but it's just ludicrous.

Mom,
I shouldn't've put your address as the return address on all my letters.
Honestly, I thought you guys would've moved by now.
I was hoping the new residents
would pretend the letters were for them.
This is for you: I will never spread your ashes. I can't.

To _____,
I forgot your name last night. Honestly.
I thought objectively about you, us, who we were.
Here's what I considered:
There is nothing more important than honest happiness.
We should get coffee and catch up.
I've addressed this to the city of Toledo
and drew a picture of your face from fifth grade on the face of the pictured mountains
I hope it finds you.

For Earth,
I've begun feeling that I can't find all your creases
but I still love your face. I think your left cheek

just below the eye-socket
is my favorite place. I might settle in North Carolina
or The Painted Hills with my parents.

How To Be a Lobster

After four months, what I had learned about Japan was as follows: the general clockworks of the culture were not designed for me. As a conversational English teacher, I had to be available when the Japanese weren't working, and if the sun was up on a weekday they were always working. This meant my nights and weekends generally belonged to high school kids and salary men, and Tuesday, when they were busy, became my new Saturday. My old Saturday was when the Japanese stuff you read about in *Lonely Planet* happened—cherry blossom festivals, tea ceremonies, et cetera—and I was never available to see them.

On Tuesdays and Wednesdays, I generally found myself roaming in search of some dirty Japanese secret or another. There were signs outside certain places, for example, that said foreigners were not allowed inside. They were sex clubs, I discovered later. Otherwise, if the weather forbade, I holed up in my tiny apartment to read, or watch movies, or try to decipher Japanese game shows.

That's the way it was, at least, for the first few months. I had arrived in November, and in early March, at the internet cafe—a place, like many, which charged for time, not beer or activities—a man called out to me as I was being escorted to my seat, a small sofa in the corner which was my usual. His voice was gruff, and upon it was a very un-Japanese "Heyyyyyyy! You!"

I stopped, blinked at him, pointed to myself.

"Oh, yeah! Um, excuse me. Are you. American?"

I wasn't sure if I should be today, but I nodded.

"Please! Sit with me. Have wine!" He held up a carafe of red wine.

This was unusual. Most of the time in this small town—small by *their* standards—the citizens eyed me with fear, contempt, or a clumsy curiosity satiated by hi and nice to meet you. I was an exotic animal, a bear in the Smokies, gawked at and generally left alone. Aside from lessons, no Japanese said more to me than "I like to speak English" because that was the extent of their speaking any English. Awkward smiles followed awkward bowing without apparent end. It was also unusual because this apparently middle-aged man—later he'd tell me he was thirty-five—was not donning a suit and tie and bad haircut. In a tee-shirt, open cotton button-up and holey jeans, this man was flanked by younger hipsters, one male and one female, also visibly awed by his forwardness. His eyeglasses were tinted, his insistence aggressive, irresistible.

His name was Shinohiro Kobayashi, he told me as he poured me a glass of wine. It was noon, but I'd found the Japanese relationship with alcohol was far less regulated than what I was used to. He offered me a cigarette, which I declined. I told him my name was Jake. His English wasn't perfect, but it got the job done far more effectively than the versions most of my students came up with. "You call me Hiro," he said. "I need American friend. Jake! We be friends, okay?" I nodded. I supposed I could be that. I didn't know anybody. I told him I could use a Japanese friend, that everybody I knew so far in Numazu was English or Australian, and that we tended to walk the town at night like a pack of coyote.

"Um, excuse me. Um, I'm sorry?"

"Oh nothing," I said. "It's alright." Already I feared we may have reached his English limits. I knew very little Japanese beyond thank you and excuse me and please. My general mode of communication involved pointing and smiling. I was surprised how that can get you by.

Hiro told me he'd spent a fair amount of time in the States, in sporadic three-month stints in Las Vegas. The US tourist visa expires after ninety days, and he spent that time entering poker tournaments. "I love America. I want live there. Maybe you help me." Now this part was typical. No Japanese ever spoke to me without wanting something, but most of the time it was free English practice. I told him the best I could do was help him with his English. "Yeah," he nodded. "No problem! I teach you Japanese."

And just like that a friendship was born. We exchanged numbers, and I figured this exchange would be as meaningless as it was at home, two strangers promising to call one another and never doing it. But he did call, the very next week, and invited me to dinner at his apartment. "I pick up you," he said. His wife, Yuki, prepared nabe, a traditional Japanese stew. She was stubby, friendly, crooked-toothed, sweet. One snooty old housewife I had been teaching told me the people of Numazu had a country look. I assumed this was what she meant. I accepted Yuki's nabe, which like most Japanese food I found awful. But I ate anyway, didn't want to be insulting. They had a good laugh at my inability to sit cross-legged, to use chopsticks. I lounged back on my hands like some Roman senator, and asked for a fork. But there were no forks in the place, just toothpicks, which I used to stab the potatoes and vegetables. I was a kind of stray animal Hiro had brought home with him. He had invited friends over—the ones from the cafe—who just as they had before sat wide-eyed, speaking only to Hiro in Japanese, and obviously regarding me. "They can't believe it!" he said. "They can't believe you are in my house! They never talk to gaijin before." And they still hadn't talked to one, using Hiro as their language filter.

The night wound down, and everyone was drunk. I didn't know where I was, if the train station was nearby. "Jake!" Hiro said. "You sleep here. I can't drive. Too much drinking." I supposed I had no other option. Yuki unrolled a futon, brought me a pillow.

Dreading as I eyed my bed for the night, Yuki appeared again behind me, holding a towel. "Please," said Yuki, "you take shower." She wasn't, as I feared, suggesting I needed one. The custom is to shower before bed to get the stink of the world off and keep it out of their beds. Getting the first shower was Japanese hospitality. Just wished the shower hadn't been basically in the kitchen.

Afterward, as they slid open the door to their bedroom, which was attached to the living room as in my place, I saw a small toddler dreaming on the family futon. "My um, daughter, Nana," said Hiro. "Uh, Nana means seven, my lucky number!" Just about everything Hiro said had an exclamation point.

For the next three months Hiro monopolized my weekends. He'd pick me up, take me somewhere, and one Tuesday, as the neon and concrete world passed me by on the wrong side of the car, I wondered why his weekends were in the middle of the week, too. I asked him about his job. "I am, uh, event analyzer," he said. I nodded, pretended I understood that, but then decided to clarify.

"So, you throw parties? Conferences? Like, for a big company?

"No," he said, pulling into a local supermarket I hadn't seen before to pick up provisions for dinner. "So, Saturday, in spring and summer, there are very much...festi-vahls! I go to man, he say you can be here, and I, cooking. But um, me, no cooking. I pay stupid kid for cooking. I take money. It's good job! I can be casual! You know Bryan Adams? Summer of '69, my favorite song. My birthday year." Hiro changed subjects often, as though there were no space between his thoughts or need to expound.

It must have been a good job he had because each week Hiro brought some hidden and expensive part of Japan out of hiding for me. He always paid, always insisted. We visited hostess bars where young Filipino women in sequined dresses danced and poured drinks for us, wiped our sweaty brows, danced and sang for us, lit men's cigarettes. But no nudity. No funny business allowed. Weird I thought, or maybe I was weird here. We went everywhere—to bars and sushi places and ramen joints and hot spring hotels—and he paid for it all. "You no need money," he'd say. "I pay." This, because of what I'd learned from the culture, seemed like systematic indebtedness, like one day I'd owe him something big, and I wondered if I'd be able to pay. I'd try to deny him paying for things, but he'd not allow it, and periodically, I'd have him and his family over to my place and make them chili or some other American dish as best as I could with the ingredients available, illiterate as I was and unable to read packaging or be sure what exactly I was buying. I introduced Hiro to tequila, and he could handle it about as well as I could shochu. He left my apartment that night singing and swaying like an idiot.

One Tuesday he called me up, said he wanted to go to a spa in Fuji City. "Very nice," he said. "You take bath in Chinese tea. It's good for health."

A half-hour beyond the concrete, the rows of tea leaves and soy beans stretched out from the base of the mountain. There were soil and grass in Japan after all, I thought, and here people actually have yards. In a little green hatchback he paid a hundred bucks for—his wife drove the new family car, complete with mini-disc player where I was used to a backup tape deck being—we rounded the curve of some impossibly narrow road. "Road in Japan," he said, very small. Um, small? What word?" From a wide placement he brought his hands near to one another.

"Narrow," I said.

"Narrow," he repeated.

Inside the spa I learned it's weird being a naked alien. I stood there a white giant, the only one of my kind. Hiro was very casual about the whole thing, dropped his shorts and held his tiny towel in front of him. I just did whatever he did, tried not to look around much, kept my eyes on the ground and followed the public spa protocol of showering beforehand. We hit the sauna, steamed ourselves red and then afterward froze our giblets off in water that was very recently ice atop Mount Fuji. Later, after sampling every variety of bath in the place—some with lavender, others with tea or menthol or a small electric current running through—and showering again, this time sitting ass out on puny toddler stools, we headed back to the locker room. Hiro stepped naked onto a small wooden board, placed his feet over an outline of feet, within which were little rounded wooden pegs. He explained that, while standing, if you felt no pain, then you were healthy. "This is, uh, feet doctor!" About two seconds was all he could stand. "Itai!" he shouted and pointed to his liver. "Too much drinking." I was able to stand on it as if the board were flat, and I felt no urgency to jump off. Hiro mewed with approval. "Oh! You are good health."

As we sat getting dressed, Hiro directed my attention to the spa entrance. An old man was disrobing, and when he peeled off his shirt he revealed a large and ornate tattoo on his back. It was intricate, expensive-looking, a web of roses and fish. "So, him. Mafia."

I had gathered that already. The *Yakuza* were part of the gaijin folklore one heard nearly upon arrival. *Welcome to Japan. Here's a weird vending machine with nothing you'll ever guess right. And here's how to spot a gangster: one can tell them apart from the general population by hipster attire and tattoos.* At the hot spring resort Hiro had taken me to with his family, there was a sign outside barring tattooed guests. Here at the Fuji City spa, I now looked more carefully around the room. A couple more men were either taking off or putting on, and only now I noticed their backs were also tattooed. Suddenly it dawned on me I was in a Japanese gangster spa. I had to catch my breath. The hell was I doing here?

"He is retired," Hiro continued, referring back to the old man. "His little finger? Cut!" Hiro made a chopping gesture. I glanced only a moment, like I wasn't looking, but I couldn't see it. "Yeah," said Hiro holding up his pinky, "me too." What an observant person would have noticed earlier, I was seeing for the first time. And my world changed instantly. The tip of his little finger wasn't missing. *It was leaning to the right.* I searched his back. There was nothing. "I no have tattoo," he said. "I do business. If tattoos, man say no business!"

Suspicious, and with the tone of a concerned wife, I asked him what happened to his finger.

"I tell boss I want retire," said Hiro. "But he say no! And my finger, cut! I pick up, and, eh--" he made his hands into a cup, "and eh, I get ice, go hospital! Doctor, with the, uh, needle," he made a sewing motion, "put back. Oh, Jake! Very expensive!" Hiro pulled up his jeans, buttoned them. I sat there stunned. No wonder he never seemed to be working, I thought. No wonder he had so much cash on hand.

I became selfish quick. "Is it okay that I'm here?" I asked him.

"Oh yeah! No problem. Some, ah, old men, don't like gaijin, but you are Hiro's guest. Heyyyyy," he said, rubbing my shoulder. "Relax!" This was the purpose of our coming here, I thought, to relax, but he just killed it. My muscles were tighter than before.

He dropped me off at my apartment later, and I sat there awed and giddy. Totally unbelievable, but I wouldn't tell anyone anyway. I'd been warned earlier by other expatriates about how foreigners would wander into the wrong bar, get slapped with a ridiculous bill, and if they couldn't pay it would receive a beating. The Yakuza were right-wingers, loyal to Japan and its culture, considered themselves replacements for Samurai. But Hiro was careful to maintain a non-Yakuza persona, and he didn't seem in the least violent. He was funny, infectious, a family man. He liked foreigners.

Only one time did I see him angry. At his apartment, after a short phone call I couldn't understand beyond the gruff tone of it, Hiro paced the tatami red faced and cursing. His breath exited him like the hissing of tractor-trailer hydraulics. Someone owed him money. "You stay here," he said to me. "I go get money. Maybe some fighting. But, uh, no problem! You stay here. You and Nana play. I come back and we. Drinking!" About an hour later, he came back with a sixer of beer and his money, and about him was the air of someone who had taken care of some menial responsibility, a dispute with the phone company now resolved, a run to the post office. He cracked open a beer, handed me one. In seconds, Hiro's can was empty. He looked at me as I nursed mine. "Jake! Too slow! Drink!" And I did as he said.

One Tuesday, as we gorged on Korean barbeque, Hiro had some news for me. He was going to ask to retire again. This seemed a dangerous idea to me, and Hiro said it was dangerous. There had been some controversy among his team—in Japan, there are teams, not families—because the second in command recently had been arrested. Now the rest of the team was expected to pitch in for his legal defense, and the boss had tapped Hiro to fill in for the newly incarcerated. "Boss want me to be new number two," he said, "but I don't want. So tonight I go to Tokyo. And all team drinking, and girls," he pantomimed drinking with one hand, tweaking nipples with the other. "And I pay. Maybe five..." He pulled over a napkin, drew zeroes with his finger. "One, two, three, four, five zero. What number?"

"Five hundred thousand," I said, converting yen to dollars and settling on five grand.

"And then I tell boss I want retire. And tomorrow, maybe no finger. Or floating. Tokyo Bay." It occurred to me he often put his exclamation points in the wrong places. That sentence needed one. He said all that, as I gulped down my lunch, with the casual air of one recounting some unusual event at the office, and with a slight chuckle on his voice I found more than unnerving. I sat back enthralled, told him I hoped he'd be okay. "Jake! Maybe this is goodbye lunch!" He threw his head back and laughed. "Kampai!"

But he was okay, and I found myself caring. I called him as soon as I got up the next morning, my stomach doing somersaults. I had genuine concern for him, but also feared I would I be questioned in this murder. But no answer, and he wouldn't answer till around noon. Hiro explained he was able to buy his way out, that he put up the equivalent of a million dollars toward his previous boss's defense. They found this acceptable in lieu of a finger, in lieu of death, especially since that was every last bit of money in a joint account. "But, no problem," he said. "I have secret money. I take money at fest-ee-vahls, and take to bank. We share! But I don't give all money. Am I a stupid? I take just little for me, take to other bank. Jake! Secret!" He placed his finger against his lips and shushed.

One morning in late June I woke up cooking in my own fat due to a four-in-the-morning sunrise, and I hadn't heard from Hiro in weeks. I generally could count on him to call me on Tuesday morning, and off we'd go on some adventure. After his retirement I found myself always a little worried for him and wondering how he'd get by. He had brainstormed about creating a sort of personal Vegas escort service for Japanese tourists, but he had a reputation problem. He went down to the police station, told them to take his name off the gangster list officially, that he was done. It's still possible, I thought, he's dead or in jail. As I poured my coffee, my mobile rang. It was Hiro. "Moshi moshi," I answered.

Hiro sounded like he'd been up for days and chain-smoking. He informed me he hadn't slept well, but I got the impression it wasn't because of the heat. I was just about to chide him about not calling me when he broke in with an apology. "I want to say I'm sorry to you."

"What for, Hiro?"

"Uh, what…um…what-for?" Probably the first time he'd heard the phrase.

"Why," I said. "Why do want to say you're sorry?"

"Oh, um, because. Lately. I was busy, you know? Trying to make company, find job. Too much thinking."

"Oh yeah?"

"Yeah!" confirmed Hiro, as though I doubted, and the word came out of him comically stretched into a crescendo at the end, as though a TV camera had zoomed in on his incredulous face just as he performed his catchphrase. "Always thinking! So I don't see you. Now, maybe okay."

I tried to imagine what he had been doing for three weeks. I saw him sitting cross-legged and half-naked on a single tatami mat, his eyes closed, working out the problems of the world—the problems of *his* world—in silence. I imagined Yuki on the other side of the sliding door, changing Nana's diapers, or with her head on her knees, wondering what to do. "No problem, Hiro-san. I know you've had a lot on your mind."

"Yeah, so. I retire from mafia," I knew this already, "and can't find job. Because nobody want. 'Oh, Kobayashi-san,' boss say, 'your name is no good.' And I say, 'Yeah, I know! But finished!'" The last time I talked to him, Hiro had just returned from an interview. He wore a white tee-shirt, ripped up jeans, and sunglasses, and he told me he asked the interviewer if he minded him smoking, and then offered him a cigarette. *No, thank you*, he said. Hiro leaned back, smiling as though he understood the absurdity of it. I wanted to tell him there's a certain etiquette in job hunting, but I knew it wouldn't do any good. Anyway, he switched subjects. "And always me and Yuki fighting," he continued. "Trying to make company. But-ah, home is no good! My house. Like World War III. I don't tell her about secret money. Maybe she get job!"

A couple of times when I had been to their apartment, it was easy to sense Yuki and Hiro were pacing the edges of some potential brawl. "Always she shop!" complained hero, and they kept their grudges charged up, ready to pop. There were times I felt they treated me like a referee, or some kind of buffer to their polemic potentialities. I felt it best not to get involved. On this morning, though, I said, "Wakata-yo!" assuring him I understood. "No problem." I didn't mention every other woman he'd fooled around with in the few months I'd known him. Not that he'd tried to hide his running around. Sometimes, it was like he was trying to impress me, and he would have, had he been single.

"So, today," Hiro continued. "I want talk to you. No, I *need* talk to you. Long time."

Something in his voice was distant, a tenuous tenor traveling from parts of him that were mostly private. There was often this paradox with him: his apparent openness was belied by half-statements made while drinking, stuff he wouldn't elaborate on but always hinted at darker hauntings within. His true love, the one after his first wife and before Yuki, died in a fire. That was all I knew, and the day he told just that much he teetered cautiously along the plank of full confession, but when merely the edge of a tear came into view, he jumped off topic. Today he wanted to talk, and there was still so much I didn't know, so much I was eager to understand and write down. Of course, I told him, I had absolutely nothing to do.

"Let's bar-b-QUE!" he trumpeted, and there it was, that Fred Flintstone way of turning up his last syllable into a riot, a yabba-dabba-do that made him so infectious, and more like the Hiro I had gotten to know. "Sembon beach. And uh, beer, and shochu. You and me, eating."

"Okay."

"And, uh, drinking!"

"Sounds good."

"And talking."

It was funny, I thought, how close I lived to the ocean, and I had seen it about as much as I'd seen good hamburgers. The people of Numazu hardly seemed to go to the local beach either. Understandable. It looked less a beach than a rock quarry. The soft and sandy idyllic beaches were a couple of hours away, and you had to have a car to get there, down near Shimoda, where one Admiral Perry of the United States Navy first sought to bust down the doors of Japanese trade with his black ships. The Japanese seemed to love that story, recounting tales of how exotic the white man was, how tall, how blue his eyes were, that "high nose" of his.

The first time I went in search of Sembon, I hiked it in December, navigating by accident those seemingly unmarked streets, climbing a hill they called Mount Kanuki, sneaking in on a Buddhist temple, unintentionally disrupting the intense quiet there—but no one, not a soul noticed—and finally, after clumsily consulting my Japanese dictionary, figured out how to ask "what is the sea?" like some great philosophical question. They'd point in a direction, jabber about something, then point in another direction. They'd repeat, *this way for a little while and then that way and then turn right again.* Not that I understood them. I just followed the hand motions. When I grew weary of charades, I followed the palm trees. The next day, I came to class very excited to tell my students I'd seen the Pacific Ocean for the first time. Only it wasn't the Pacific, they told me, it was Saruga Bay, where fisherman brought in Numazu's famous seafood. To a Kentucky boy, it was *the Pacific.*

"Okay," said Hiro on the phone. "I pick up you, maybe ten."

No matter how many times I corrected him, proper use of prepositional verb phrases escaped him. "Hai, hai," I said. "See you then."

We drove up to that quarry of a beach, upon which was a bed of smooth gray skipping stones littered with driftwood and seaweed. Bits of newspaper swirled over aluminum cans smashed into the rocks. "Sembon is not nice beach, ne?" offered Hiro, snatching the obvious from the salty air. "But, uh, nice wind. And sun!" He gesticulated dramatically toward the cloudless sky and I lamented for a moment the absence of sunscreen with SPF greater than thirty. At the grocery store, where Hiro purchased what had to be five pounds worth of various meats—chicken wings, pork slices, beef strips, little weenies, and sand dollars of some kind of olive-colored fish—and more beer and shochu than two people should be able to drink in a few hours, I made Rosetta stones of the sunscreen labels, comparing symbols and numbers. Hiro sort of jack-in-the-boxed up behind me and asked, "Why you need sun lotion?"

"Haku-jin, ne? White boy," I reminded him, and I was proud of my Japanese.

"You don't need. I want see you like lobster!"

Hoping he wouldn't be granted his wish, I wavered between two bottles, both with a large number thirty on them. "Not if I can help it," I said.

"That one!" Hiro grabbed a bottle and tossed it into his basket. "Ikou!" And that was that.

On the beach the wind was fierce, pressing my shirt and shorts full against me until the outline of my body was visible. I held on to the khaki hat I'd purchased and grabbed a few plastic grocery bags.

"Oh, look!" said Hiro, pointing to a concrete pier jutting out about thirty feet into the water. Against the backdrop of ocean and sun, the horizon formed an absurdly monochrome and profound nothingness. The wind tussled some sort of raised banner above what must have been fifty Japanese in black suits and business skirts, all of them huddled impossibly close together on the pier, not unlike a waddle of penguins pushing illogically against the cold sea. They applauded and cheered at some unknown elation. "Business party," concluded Hiro. "Um, maybe boss. His birthday."

Hiro's torso disappeared into the hatchback, and he pulled more stuff than I thought possible out of his green clown car: two folded-up lawn chairs, a Styrofoam cooler, a case of Draft One, a bag of ice, and what looked like a white bucket with a rust-colored metal screen. I asked him what it was.

"This is, um, for meat cooking. What name?"

"A grill, I think."

"*Goo-ree-ooh.*"

"Grill."

"Goo-reel."

"Grill."

"Grell."

"Close enough. But I've never seen one like that."

"Yeah! It's small. Very *portable.*"

I smiled and shook my head at his strange vocabulary. He knew words like "tandem" and "straight flush" but struggled over the basics like "pencil" or "red." My Japanese was like his English, forged through need-to-know and not through studying. I could rattle off words and phrases like "wisdom tooth" (o-ya-shirazu) and "Don't mess with me!" (namen-ja-nezo) but couldn't for the life of me remember colors or their crazy-ass number system. Cylinder-shaped things had different number words than flat things, which had different number words than for fish or rabbits, which had different number words than for glass objects, and so on, or so I was told.

It took two trips to fully set up camp there about ten yards from the tide. I set up the chairs, filled the cooler with ice and beer, and lathered myself up with sun block while Hiro scoured the beach for paper and driftwood. He came back with a pile of litter, stripped the wood apart and crumpled up the paper, and carefully placed the pieces inside the bucket grill, which he was shielding from the wind with his back as he tried to light it. Once he got the fire going, he leaned back from it, looked up at me in my canvas chair, and took off his tinted prescription glasses that made him look bad-ass at all times of day. He wiped the sweat from his forehead. "Japan is, uh, sultry!" he said.

"Not sultry. Humid."

"Humid?"

"Hot and wet."

"Right, sultry," he said with a confident nod.

"Not sultry."

"Humid, da ne?"

"Right."

"What mean sultry?"

"Hot and wet, but different. It's like sex. This isn't. Humid is better."

"Japan is humid." He rolled it around in his mouth as though not sure if he liked the taste of it, and not quite mastering the hard H or the *yoo* sound together. It sounded more French the way he said it, more like *oo-mid.*

"Really, really, wet-blanket stinkin' humid," I said. "But it's not so bad here on the beach."

"Okay!" Hiro interjected as though he had grown tired of the English lesson. " Let's Bar-B-QUE!" The yabba-dabba-do again, with his trademark quick switch of subject. He handed me a beer from the cooler and grabbed one for himself, and soon after came the *crack* of the opening ceremony. "Jake," he said, smiling as though we were celebrating, "kampai!"

"Cheers, Hiro," I echoed as we clunked cans together. I took a sip and placed the beer in the chair's cup holder. With the canvas hat pulled tight around my scalp, I fished out a cigar I'd been saving for the right occasion. Sitting on the beach doing nothing but eating and drinking seemed to me like cause for smoking a nice, big stogie, so I fired one up, looked at Hiro with it clinched between my teeth. I felt like an old-world gangster.

"Oh! Like a gentleman!"

"Tanksh," I said from behind my cigar, and Hiro already was crushing an empty beer can.

He looked at me suspiciously as I nursed my first beer the way I always did. Here came our usual ritual. "Jake! Drink! Drink, drink, drink!" he commanded in a way I knew was not negotiable.

So I choked it down, belching between gulps, crushed the can and reached for another. This was our custom – drinking quickly and not stopping until we were sloshed beyond repair. He would accept no less. "Sorry, man. I'm not a professional like you," I'd say to him, every time we were together.

Hiro reached into the bag of chicken wings and placed them in a careful arrangement on the grill. His eyes, I noticed not for the first time through the cracks at the sides of his glasses, were a faint yellow, an ancient map with bloodshot trade routes to his brown corneas. The first time I'd noticed them was at the gangster spa where we would be, to my completely uncomfortable Southern chagrin, naked as jaybirds among a non-English-speaking pack of tattooed hooligans.

I was on my third beer when the chicken wings were finished. Hiro tonged them onto a paper plate weighted down with one of the billions of rocks at our feet. "Hai, dozo," he said, and I took a bite.

"Oishi, Hiro! Really good." This guy could cook anything, and took pride in his ability to bring out the full flavor of food. His culinary skill was learned during his early mafia days, when, as a fledgling, he was assigned to the festival booths as a cook, paid with lodging and two rice balls a day.

As I was busy gnawing at the meat on my plate, Hiro (finally!) announced why he had brought me here. "So, I want to talk about dream. Dream is, uh, important!" I noticed again how nearly everything Hiro said was punctuated, and he looked at me as though waiting for me to say something else. "Right?" he asked, and I nodded. "What your dream?" And he crushed another beer can.

I squinted at him and grinned before clarifying. "Like a sleeping dream?"

He paused, considered it, shook his head violently. "No, not sleeping dream. Big dream. Like plan. What your dream? You tell me."

Nodding in agreement, I kept my English easy, knowing what I was about to say was vastly oversimplified. "Oh, you know, that's a good question. My dream is maybe hard to understand. My dream is too big, Hiro. Maybe impossible – maybe, I can't have it. My family, my mom and dad, want me to work for a big company, right? Like those people on the pier on the boss's birthday. And marry a rich girl. We call it 'the American Dream' – you know," I enumerated on my fingers, "job and wife and nice house and two kids and two cars and all that shit.

"My brother, he works for a big company. He makes a lot of money, and I think he does bad things to get it. He works only for the company, and he doesn't think maybe it's not okay what he does. His only dream is money. But me, Hiro, I'm different. I want something else, something beautiful I don't have to be a bad man to get. I have my own crazy thoughts, you know? I try to be scientific and logical about life because I think that's what a man should be, but recently I've started to believe in things that are just pretend, just my imagination, probably. I've started to *believe* in them, Hiro, because strange things have happened, things I thought were impossible. It's like magic, like lightning in my hands." I paused for a drink, wondered if he understood all that. "When I was kid I wanted to be Indiana Jones. You know Indiana Jones?"

"Da da-da! Da da-da da!" he sang out the theme song. "Harrison Ford!"

"Right. Well, it's kind of like believing you're Indiana Jones, but Indiana Jones isn't real, right? I still want to be him, but he is not real. Wakaru?"

"I understand," said Hiro, pushing through a swallow.

"And maybe none of what happened to me before I came to Japan was real, but I want it to be. Sometimes I think I've lost my mind, that I'm crazy, but if I'm not crazy, and all of it was real, then life is beautiful and worth living. That's why my girl back home, that's why she is important. She makes me into Indiana Jones, and because of that I saw my whole life in her, my kids, too. It's funny, you know, funny strange, and I was scared. I ran away because I knew meeting Jillie was the end of me as one person, and sometimes a dream coming true is scary—and complicated. I came to Japan because I had only seen Kentucky. And Kentucky is a very small place, very beautiful land, but the people there, they don't know the world and couldn't tell me about it. They know their home and they are happy with it. But Jillie, I knew she was the one, that she was the last woman. But I wanted to see the world first. So strange! I knew she was the one. I knew because her soul – you know the word *soul*?"

Hiro's face screwed up into a deflated *O*. "Soul." He considered it. "Soul? Jake, I don't know *soul*."

A vocabulary lesson. A hard one. Like trying to explain the ocean with tear drops. "Um, soul is, inside." I pointed to my abdomen. "Not stomach or liver." I made a V with my hands pointed toward my gut. "Soul is not rock, or wood…It's nothing, but it's something, you can't see it." This wasn't working. He was clearly lost. "When you die, soul is your ghost."

"Oh! Like spirit," he said, as if it were obvious that was the word I needed.

"Exactly. Jillie's spirit was the same as my spirit." I pondered what I just said. "Ahhh! I sound crazy. Anyway, she told me we had lived before, that we were married in the past, in lives before this life—we were married, we died, we were born again, we loved again. Again and again we have done this. And that is crazy talk. But I think I believe her. It's a beautiful story."

Though I worried he understood none of that, Hiro grew excited, like the kid in class with his hand always raised. "Oh! Not crazy. Because. Sometimes, I think to me. I think you, maybe, brother in different place. In America, sometimes, before, you and me are brothers." He sank his face in the can.

Everybody's gone crazy, I thought, Hiro too, and maybe it was my fault. I had often pondered out loud the questions of my soul, perhaps put ideas into his head. I remembered one night at his apartment, while we drank, he stared a while at me and then announced to Yuki my aura—my "atmosphere"—was yellow. But at the beach I mentioned none of it, and I just said, "Okay, good. You know what I mean. So, my dream is to go home to Kentucky, write books and make babies with her. Sounds like the perfect life to me: beautiful stories and babies. And I want to build a house somewhere south or west, because I don't like winter. And I want to be rich, in money and in family…but not yet, and I have no idea how to get the money without betraying myself. All I know is I want Jillie in my life." I looked at him. He said nothing. "Wakaru?"

Hiro's nodding head was bending up and down like a thoroughbred's as he stared down at the rocks considering. When he finished, he looked up suddenly as if waking from a daydream. "Oh, Jake! Nice dream! Gambatte! Good luck. One day I hope. My family, and uh, your family, barbeque at your house. In Kentucky."

A nice thought, but it didn't seem likely. I couldn't imagine it. But I said instead, "That sounds good to me, Hiro. Cheers to that." And I chugged a fourth beer. "Your turn."

He settled into his seat and looked out at the ocean. The sun beat down full force on my arms and legs as the wind stripped the empty paper plate from my hand and sent it off down the rocky beach. A swarm of dragonflies, a number larger than in any collection of flying things I'd ever seen, came whipping down the shoreline, all in line, all in purpose, ignoring us and buzzing on like a blur of helicopters off to war. Hiro laid out the little fish discs on the grill. "Yeah, so, high school. I don't like study. Only soccer. And uh, my. Hometown. Shizuoka is famous soccer town. I want to be *pro-fessional*! But, my knees, you know? No good! My father said, you need study! But I don't like. Most times, I don't go to school. My dad's friend was. Pub owner. So I tell Mom. And Dad. I go to school, but no school, pub. Drinking, and uh, smoking. And later, you know, I was mafia. Because, good money, and people give me respect. But I don't like mafia. I played *guitar*. I want to be a singer, or maybe movie maker. Heh. I was. Kid! I don't know what I want. And then, jail," he held up two fingers, "two years."

This was the way he always told stories—tacking on some major life event like it's just a necessary addendum, a footnote to more important things. *I didn't like school. I liked playing soccer and guitar, and drinking and partying. Later I joined the mafia, and then I was in jail for two years. The end.* He'd mentioned his stint in jail before, but never had elaborated. I asked him once, and he just said he did something bad, but the judge understood and went easy on him. It had something to do with his mother, he said, and defending her.

As he tended the grill and turned up his beer, Hiro went on like that, bouncing from story to story, from small event to huge event as if they were even on some whacked-out scale. I chewed on every piece of flesh he put on my plate, and tossed back cans of Draft One as the redness crawled up my legs like a pox. He talked about cutting hair at his parents' barbershop, losing his virginity at thirteen to the babysitter next door, the pack of Akitas they kept in their house, a twelve-year-old daughter he hadn't seen in years, $50,000 poker tournaments in Vegas, cooking at local festivals, shooting up a rival team's apartment building with an Uzi, his mother's death, his father's death, his uncle's death, an underage Kentucky girl—*the coincidence!*—he picked up along the side of the road in Vegas who paid for her rent and food in blow jobs, and back to the tasty meat he was grilling on this humid, sunny afternoon at the beach. Sometimes I wondered if he made things up.

"I went to China," he went on, "and saw the Great Wall. And it was, um, great. Very big. Amazing. And China is big country, but I don't like China. Dirty and poor and no good. At Great Wall, I said where is toilet? A man said, over there! And it's nothing. Just, um, grass. I said, I can't! But um, I have to…um, shit. So, okay I go to grass, but no paper! I said, where?" Hiro shrugged his shoulders, held his hands out in front of him. "Where is paper? The man said, you bring! Oh, I hate China!"

Of course I nearly choked. I envisioned him squatting next to a Chinese stranger in a field, pleading for toilet paper next to what is always portrayed as a marvel of human engineering. Hiro went on, as usual. "And Japan, you know. Always I look at ocean." He stretched out his hand toward the horizon. "Japan is too small. And now. Japan is no good. Can't get dream." He reached into the air grasping at the wind, and he tightened his voice into a note high and pleading, "Hey! Dreams! Come back!" The sight of him was more comical than the words suggested. He cocked his head and chuckled. "In Japan, no one has dream. I went to Grand Canyon. I thought, ohhhh, America is very big, you know. Big roads and big cars. I rented. Convertible! I am thinking, oh! I want come here. I want Nana live here. Women in Japan. No chance, because can't!" Hiro made an X with his hands and frowned.

He was never a softer man than when he spoke of his daughter. If there ever was any real love in him, it was for Nana. And the idea that Nana would be reduced to the status that he himself put upon women, even to a worse degree than most, was sad to him. If Nana followed the rules, she'd go to college, become a secretary and hope to be married by an ambitious salaryman so she could stop working and get with the babymaking. But she shouldn't expect a faithful, or even present, husband. "My dream," he said, "I want move to America. Make company."

I noticed again the redness on my legs, and when I sensed a break in his speech I pleaded that we remove ourselves from the relentless onslaught of the sun. "Gambatte, Hiro. I hope so. Gawd! Look at my legs. We need to go soon. This sunscreen doesn't work, I think."

"Not-yet-toh," he objected. "We need more talking." *He* needed more talking. I was being cooked like that insane amount of meat he bought. But I knew it wouldn't do any good to protest, not when he was fixated on some vague purpose of his. And he was my ride. I sulked a little and sipped at my beer. "Drink! Drink! Drink!" he said, and automatically I started into a full gulp at his command. It perturbed me a little that I followed his orders without thinking like that, but there was always something very commanding about him, something in his presence precluding rejection. "You know," he began again, "you and me meeting, only chance, like miracle!"

"Guuzen," I corrected.

"Not guuzen! Not coincidence. Miracle! And now you, like my little brother." He smiled at me in that innocent, eyebrow-raised way that transformed him from bad-ass to pussycat. He took a puff off of a cigar I had given him earlier and continued smiling. I smiled back. I couldn't help it. "So, da ne?" Hiro said.

"Okay, yeah. Like my big brother."

"So, so, so, so." The party on the pier had long since dissolved as the salarymen and secretaries in their black suits took down their happy birthday banners and trudged back to the office. They were replaced by a tall white man in a yellow thong, sunning himself. Must be European, I thought.

Hiro began again. "So last month, I went to doctor." And right away I knew something was up. He never went to the doctor; he hated them. "It was secret. I don't tell Yuki. I had…health check! Tell him check all body because I feel no good. One morning, I look at mirror, and my eyes—small, and, tired. And my shoulder—pain. And breathing—no good. So I think, mmhmm, maybe! And I had test. And uh, my uh," he made an outline with his fingers on his chest in the pattern of his lungs.

"Your lungs?"

"Yeah! Lungs. My lungs, no good. Doctor say to me, five years, forty years old, maybe. Dead." His casual, light-hearted certainty I found confusing. There was no difference in his tone, no hint of sadness to match what he had just told me. He said it in much the same way he said everything else that day. He arched his eyebrows. "Wakatta?"

"Maybe I understand. Tell me again." I swigged my beer, hoping I'd heard differently.

"Yeah so, my uh," he made the outline again.

"Lungs."

"Lungs. No good. Doctor say can't. Operate. So, five levels. I am level three. So I'm. Dead. Maybe five years." And he lined up the weenies on the grill.

I braved into the wind between us. "Cancer?"

"Yeah," he said, the least triumphant of all the yeahs so far. "Cancer. Here." He made a circle around the upper right portion of his chest. I lit a cigarette, feeling loose and drunk, not knowing what to say. "I tell doctor, I don't want medicine. It's okay! My father dead. Forty-six. My uncle dead. Forty-two. So me: forty. I know before. I tell doctor, I can't stop smoking. If drinking, no problem. But smoking, *can't.*" Hiro lowered his shoulders from the final shrug of that last appeal and took another puff off his cigar.

I kept my silence, looking up into the ether trying to find the words, groping the wind for them the same way Hiro had reached for his dreams. I couldn't find a damn thing to say. My best friend in Japan just told me, with such nonchalance, that he was dying.

"But uh, no problem," said Hiro, over-annunciating the *em* on the end of problem. "I like short and big. Because, if too long and uh, semai...what word, you said?"

"Narrow."

"Yeah. If too long and. Narrow. No good story. My life, good story. I need you to write, make book."

The gravity of what he expected took a minute to press hard enough onto my body for me to feel it. Hiro had just commissioned me to write his life story, a helluvan honor and one helluva presumption. But I said nothing. Just looked down at the rocks, back up to him. He continued to turn the weenies, tasted a sample. "Oishi! Try!"

The sausage was still red hot, and I was quick about scooping what I'd bitten off away from my tongue and tossing it on the plate. "Really good, Hiro. You're an excellent chef." That's what I said, though I knew they were only weenies. The questions started stacking in my mind.

"Oh, Jake! Your legs are very red."

"Uh-huh. So, when are you going to tell Yuki?"

"Um, never," he offered up with the high, almost question-like pitch of a punch line, smiling. "Like a cat. Go to forest, or somewhere, with no people. Die with me only." When this guy wasn't making you laugh, or hurting somebody, he was the saddest thing in the world.

"I'm so sorry, Hiro."

"Yeah. No problem. Men. In my family. Short life. I need you. Now, I only need laugh."

"I'll try," I said with sudden lack of faith in myself. Squatting there, like a toad in my mind, was one of those funny, and ugly, juxtapositions croaking out from wherever funny and ugly juxtapositions like to croak. I thought of—for the first time in years—a pair of game-winning lay-ups I missed in the McKinney County Sixth Grade Basketball Championship.

"Thank you," he said. Hiro swigged, put his eye up to the opening. The beer, all of it, was finished, and he opened up the bottle of shochu. Suddenly, I knew we weren't leaving any time soon. There was still a lot of meat left to anchor us down in the wind and alcohol to drown ourselves in. He dropped some pork onto my plate and poured some shochu into a plastic cup. "Dozo," he said, and I thanked him even though I was stuffed full as a tick in a blood mobile and drunker than a frat house pledge. He put more chicken wings on the grill, and as he turned them and mooned over their bronze color, he sang to them in English: *Ohhhhhh, yessssss! You are so beautiful to me! Can't you see?*

He left the wings alone and took a drink of shochu. Looking again out on the ocean, Hiro grew serious, pensive. "Life is like. Wind," he said, his English suddenly very good. "You can't fight wind." He put his hand upright and held it against the breeze. "If like this. See, my hand. If like this, can't move. And if try to move, then, fall reverse!" He let his hand fall backward and the wind take it over his shoulder. "But if like this," he flattened his hand so his fingers formed an aerodynamic wing slicing through the wind and let it glide like that, "then can move. This is good."

I smiled at him because I had thought of something, a way to make good on the responsibility he assigned to me earlier. "Are you changing your name to Buddha, Hiro-san?" I effected the lotus position, closed my eyes and grinned stupidly.

He looked a little stunned, cocked his head and then, "Ha! Ha, ha! Ah-hoowa, hoowa, hoowa!" He choked himself laughing. "Oh, Jake, too funny! Don't make me laugh!" He pointed to the side of his chest. "Pain!"

"Doctor's orders, man."

He smiled at me, that boyish grin, still lightly coughing. "So, da ne?"

It was approaching three in the afternoon, and I was as red as a turnip. It was clear we weren't leaving until the food was gone, which wouldn't be for another couple of hours at least. So I had an idea I should have had earlier, and got up with the intention of going to the car to get the extra pair of shorts and the shirt I brought with me in case, like so many Tuesday nights, I ended up staying at Hiro's. Figured I could use them for cover.

But here's the thing about shochu, or Japanese booze in general: If you drink it while sitting down, you don't really feel all that drunk. In fact, you feel damn lucid, and getting up seems like the easiest thing in the world to do. However, as a foreigner will notice on his first Friday night in Japan, as the salarymen wobble by on what were, in Japanese, called baby bird legs, walking is a surprisingly difficult matter. Add a strong gust of wind and you're screwed.

I managed to stagger my way to the car, lean into the hatch without toppling into it, and wagged my way back to where we were sitting. With my forearms already covered by a tee-shirt, I bent over to step, very carefully, one leg at a time through the second set of shorts to cover my calves and shins. And once they were covered, while I was still bent toward the ground, an extra-strength wind gale broadsided my cotton-encumbered body as though I had made sails for it to press against. The wind sent me backward, and I landed on my back with my arms and legs pointed helplessly up toward the sky.

"Ha! Hoowah! Ha hoowah! Jake!" Hiro wheezed. "Hee hee. Thank you! I need laugh! Oh, Pain! Pain!" He held his side and his chest as he laughed."Ha hoowah! You are like lobster!"

Preaching to the Converted

He claimed to have seen an owl on the train bridge at night perhaps with a hurt wing because it didn't move when he approached, but turned its head one hundred and eighty degrees then hissed like a cat or a mute expressing pure hate, and then it perched quiet and repeatedly winked. He said that during one of his many cross-country trips for who knows what reason he stopped his car in what was maybe Missouri or Kansas, got out, and walked long and steadily into a weed field unable to see what he was actually stepping in, getting into, due to darkness and thickness of vegetation and the off-key whistling of the wind probably masking the rattle-shake of rattlesnakes, partially hypnotized by the smell of pollen and fertilizer and soil soaked by humidity, to see, surrounded by darkness and obscurity, a full moon pulsing in blood red. He described in an amazing lack of detail the duration he sat on a desert denuded bluff at sunrise and watched the sun arch over Shiprock so that its shadows gave it a movement and the dry plains around it shivered in waves of heat. He claimed to have swum with a catfish that was as long as his own body in a rare deep part of the Mississippi river and that its head whiskers felt him, touched him, and he in turn stroked its smooth white milky underside. He told us these stories and more because he knew they were true and that, like him, we were so eager to simply believe.

The Smell of the Past

An Essay

"You certainly are getting all your stocking stuffers." The clerk at Target read me as a Christmas-shopping mother (OK, maybe a grandmother).

"Yes, I've got everyone covered." I played up the role, not hinting that all those boxes of cards, an orgy of cards, were for me and me alone.

Ah, you think, a story about some old lady who collects baseball cards. This is the 21st Century – that's no big deal. And it wouldn't be even when I was growing up in the 1960s (OK, now you're saying definitely grandmother). I knew girls who collected them. However, I wasn't one of them. You see, I can say that – in a 1960s boy's voice. Back then, I was a boy. Little League, Boy Scouts (briefly, mustering out with the exalted rank of Second Class), the works. A rather inept boy, but a boy nonetheless.

Only decades later would I face the truth: I needed to live on the outside as the woman I was on the inside. At age 55, I underwent a rapid transformation, rapid as such things go, transitioning from male to female, from my first appointment with a gender therapist to the date of my surgery in exactly two years. If we'd passed each other in the mall Christmas shopping and managed through the holiday daze to notice each other, you would not think twice – you'd assume I was somebody's mother...OK, maybe grandmother...doing her shopping.

Why, after all the work to deliver myself into the world, would, instead of buying clothes, jewelry, make-up, all those girly things I dreamed of doing openly, would I be dragging myself back into my baseball-carded past?

And it was the past I wanted. These weren't new cards. You can still buy unopened "wax packs" – the way they traditionally came in now-vanished wax paper wrappers – of old cards, repackaged as vintage cards with appropriate prices that definitely are not vintage. These weren't from the 1960s, but the late 1980s, the last age of the traditional Topps cards. Close enough to hearken back to my youth. But I ask again, why would I want to pull myself back to a very confusing time of my life? Back then, I knew something was deeply "wrong" with me, but I didn't know what. I played in Little League, but hated it, hated being one of the scrubs they put in right field where we could do the least damage, hated not being anywhere near the player my older brother was. Yet like any other boy of those times, I dreamed of being a big league ballplayer, dreams lifted off from baseball cards. Such contradictions tore at my young soul.

You could say I learned to read from baseball cards. I was five when I saw my first baseball card, something brought in from that mysterious world called school by my brother, a foreign place I only heard about through his tales. My mother and I would wait the sound of the bus, for him to come through the door. Sometimes he pulled some mysterious object from his Roy Rogers lunchbox. One day, like a magician, he revealed something called "a baseball card." I strained on tiptoes to see it. How he gained possession of it, I don't know, as he had no cards to trade, but behold, there it was. I don't think I was allowed to hold it, perhaps he let me briefly touch it.

I remember the card as being that of Woody Held, shortstop for our favorite team, the Cleveland Indians. As such, it would be a coveted card. How my brother wangled it from someone, to this day I cannot fathom. But that feat must have laid the foundation for his later success in the banking industry. Baseball cards, the rows of statistics on the back developed his acuity for numbers.

It took some doing – our parents did not make such major purchases lightly. Odds did not favor spending hard-earned coin on such frivolous objects. They deliberated the proposition for months, softening from a hard "no," in no hurry. Waiting, they believed was good for the young soul, at least until we wore them down. Finally it was agreed upon that, upon such and such a date, while going into town for some now-forgotten event, we would go into Newberrys dime store and purchase a minimum amount of baseball cards, in those days when a nickel bought a pack of six cards. And so it came to pass. Outside the store we opened our cards. Or rather my brother did, both of ours. As I couldn't yet read, he'd call roll as he shuffled through my cards, calling out which players were good. I waited to hear if I'd gotten a Cleveland Indian, any would do. Alas, none. He, of course, got one. Catcher John Romano – who instantly became *my* favorite player.

We slept with those cards, looking at them with our flashlights under the covers. I horribly bent Don Nottebart when I fell asleep on his card. I still have it, sharp crease down the middle, which may be symbolic of his short career. I also still have the card, nearly worn back into the pulp from which it came, of Chico Fernandez, a Cuban shortstop with Detroit, one of my favorites for some unknown reason, perhaps his friendly face, or his batter's stance, or simply that I liked the Tigers cartoon logo. I knew the player's faces as well as I did those of my relatives. And I slowly learned to read the captions under the cartoons on the back, learn what "HR" and "Ave." stood for. They were all the literature I needed.

OK, stop here; I'm gushing with nostalgia. But does it explains why I still buy them, outdated non-computerized relics of the 20th Century? Relics like the World Series itself.

The question remains, why am I nostalgic for any part of a childhood in which I was not free to be my true self? Soon after my transition from male to female, my hometown alumni association held an open house at my former grade school before the building was torn down. Standing in my first grade classroom, my first feeling was, boy, the chalk boards are a lot lower than I remember. When I looked to the coat hooks at the back of the room, it all came back, as if my jacket was hanging there. Fifty years later. The old feelings hit, of how lost, bewildered, not fitting in, tense and on guard against something,

something I didn't understand. I stood in the spot where my desk would have been, called to that boy over the decades, "Don't worry, don't be so afraid. It will turn out good. We'll get there together."

Baseball. The game was my father's first love. In most of his childhood photos, he's wearing a baseball shirt or full uniform. I wanted to please him, but I couldn't. I still see myself lost in right field dropping the ball or at the plate striking out with a weak swing, suffering anxiety and depression in an age that did not recognize anxiety and depression in children.

Yet those cards still bring forth a joy, a simple childlike pleasure, especially the old ones, hence I overpay for unopened Topps packs from the end of the age of the traditional baseball card, changed little from my youth, simple cardboard, picture on one side, statistics on the back, packed with a stick (two sticks back in my day) of bubblegum that gave them that distinctive sweet scent.

After courts struck down their near monopoly, Topps gained competition in 1981, sets put out (without bubblegum) by Fleer and Donruss, but I mark the decline in baseball cards not myself getting older but to 1989, the introduction of the first high-priced 'premium' cards by Upper Deck, high-quality photos on both sides of coated stock, selling for the outlandish price of a buck a pack, twice the price of other brands. Soon the others followed. Gone were the wax wrappers, the visceral feel of the experience. After 1991, Topps stopped packaging bubblegum with the cards (after all, who wants their valuable collectables stained by gum), gone was smell of the cards. The price of a 15-card pack of Topps rose from 59 cents in 1991 to 89 cents two years later. A glut of expensive but sterile cards followed until the baseball-card bubble, made of money not bubblegum, burst.

So I open the wax to the past. Here's Billy Ripken struggling in the shadow of his brother. Dennis Eckersley, who saved his last game long ago, still looking fierce. Gary Sheffield once more carrying the tag 'Future Star." Curt Young who will never be young again, the back of his card stained by bubblegum. So many names that reached the highest level of the game yet are now forgotten. Who is Nelson

Santovenia? He sounds like a war-torn Balkan country. One entire team now vanished – the Montreal Expos.

One thing is missing – the smell. The petrified sticks of bubblegum have lost their scent. Yes, I once tried to chew some. Don't do it at home – it crumbled in my mouth into a waxy residue. Missing the smell, I tried an experiment, sealing cards in Ziploc bags with various samples of fresh bubblegum, not just the Bazooka brand that came with the cards, but Double Bubble and Hubba Bubba. Baggies of baseball cards – like some drug dealer? Yes, I was looking for some kind of fix, but this was a scientific experiment, leaving the cards sealed with the gum for a couple days, hoping that in those hermetically sealed bags, the smell would infuse. The samples were open and sniff-tested at precisely timed scientific intervals: 36, 48, 72 hours... Results – disappointing. Alas, it just wasn't the same. Even Bazooka smelled different, too sweet. I've seen "baseball bubblegum" advertised on the internet, even baseball-card bubblegum perfume. But, yea, I've abandoned hope.

So it's true, you can't go home again. Yet for good or bad, can we ever leave? Some do, a fate far worse than nostalgia. Some do, especially amid the transsexual community, their early years filled with horrible memories, parents who tried to beat them into submitting to their birth gender, schools where they were bullied or at least forced into invisibility, non-entities. A few poor souls at the group meetings rage with anger at their past, repudiating everything about it, denying it as if to erase it. Yet the very act of doing so demonstrates they can't shake it.

Most, however, sit much more easily with who they were, slipping easily between past and present, many saying they feel at the core no different than they were before transitioning. Dinner at a restaurant after the meeting reveals an amazing mixture of selves, conversation switching from cooking to cars without shifting gears, from experiences in the military to styles of shoes without breaking stride. And yes, baseball cards.

The question should be, not why, but why not baseball cards? At last in my life I'm fused into a whole person, with nothing erased or wasted. Including my first encounters with baseball cards.

I don't open all of the old wax packs. I love holding them, remembering the moment of anticipation before tearing open the wrapper. I hold onto that moment of endless possibility. Who knows who is inside that wrapper.

Bridget's Defiance

"The ambivalence of women two generations removed
is lodged in my abdomen like a still born.
The potential threat of tepid oatmeal being abandoned on the kitchen table until noon
causes my ovaries to recede to my brain,
The vision of my wedding bed, stretched out before me a commemorative monument to the
dismissing of my quintessential nature surely would render me dead.
Hanged by the laces of work boots.

How then should I proceed?
Hysterectomy? Or a lobotomy?
Relinquish my primitive ability to reproduce?
Or eradicate any trace of linear thought?

For it is pure impracticality to assume the coexistence of both."

The Cold

Amelia quit digging in the closet when an engine revved close to the trailer. Her boyfriend, Michael, said he was selling the clothes dryer to buy propane—an act to gain temporary footing and show Amelia's mother they were serious this time about turning their lives around, enough so to maybe allow her daughter, Emily, to come for a visit. She reached up and tugged a dress from a hanger, a size seven floral that Emily could still wear. She wedged the dress into a garbage bag when the entry door thumped shut.

She stood and tucked the bag into the closet.

"Are you dead yet?" Michael said from the living room and laughed.

Amelia stomped from the bedroom holding one of Emily's red ballet flats and pointed it at him. "You damn right I'm dead, about as dead as you're in the sack."

"What?" he asked.

"Did you buy propane?"

He smiled and looked away, then dug around in his winter jacket and pulled out a glass pipe. "What propane?" He clutched a twisted cellophane wrapper between two fingers and dangled a clear rock. "You don't want any?"

When she first met Michael three years ago, he was twenty-five, two years younger than her, and had a decent job at the copper mines. In the beginning, he always put her and Emily first. He took them to county fairs and held their hands and bought them buttered popcorn and stuffed unicorns—the calluses along his hands a reminder of the deeds of man, of providing until the back gave. But then he got introduced to meth by friends. The addiction got worse and before long, there were no more trips to Lake Superior or county fairs.

Instead, they were selling TVs, stereos, sacrificing the grocery money. He lost his job (was caught blowing meth in a porta potty) and both of their complexions deteriorated—tooth decay and facial scabs—and her mother finally took notice, taking her granddaughter to live with her some fifty miles away.

Amelia sighed and shook her head, the cave of her mouth beginning to salivate at the hint of ammonia. "I wish you'd listen. When we gonna stop so we can bring Emily home?"

"We'll figure it out later. Damn." He sat on the floor cross-legged and flicked a lighter, moved the flame under the pipe's head until it glowed. "In the morning," he said, struggling to catch a whiff of smoke that escaped his mouth.

"Tomorrow," she said, and plopped down next to him. She dug a finger into dented carpet left by the TV stand while he took another drag. "She might be in college then."

"Keep it up," he said.

She massaged a blister on her lip with her tongue and scooted closer; then they passed the pipe back and forth until morning.

* * *

Outside their rental trailer, plastic window sheeting flapped in the wind, its movement as constant as the so-called buzzard dust that burned under her skin. She scratched her neck and rolled up off the living room carpet, went into the kitchen. The clock on the wall showed twelve thirty. If Emily made it to school, she would be at recess, hanging from the monkey bars or chasing some boy around the swings. Or maybe she stayed indoors today and colored a pink pony with black spots or read out of some book in her lap. When Michael returned from visiting the dealer yesterday, he said kids were being shown photographs of failed meth mothers at school, ones with scabs on their faces. He laughed and said it was part of Michigan's plan to show its effects, and that it wouldn't be long before Amelia's face covered a billboard somewhere.

Her fingers trembled as she picked a scab on her cheek the size of a penny. She moved from the stove and went back into the living room.

Michael was asleep on the floor, curled in a ball with his jacket and boots on, where the couch used to be. On most nights now they leaned against the wall, clutching the pipe. Amelia zipped up her jacket and grabbed the bag. She crept out onto the concrete blocks in front of the trailer. A light mist moistened her face as she walked toward the blacktop. The sky's dead belly rolled southward from Canada and curled above the trees like a thick muscle. She continued to distance herself from the trailer, heading east, the sleet now soaking through her jacket, seeping into her skin and bones. She wished she had an umbrella or a rain jacket, or even better a phone to call her mother to come and get her, if her mother even would. What was so difficult about trying to be normal, of having food in the refrigerator or heat circulating the trailer? Why couldn't they both have jobs or a car?

A car splashed and hissed as it sped by and she struggled to make out the driver. It was a woman with flashy earrings. Their eyes met but the lady kept going. Each time that Amelia had tried to leave, the story about the man from Baraga always resurfaced. How the man had wandered down the road high one night, apparently became disoriented, and crawled into a culvert. He wasn't found until the following spring when the snowmelt had pushed him out. It was said that he had a glass pipe in his pocket and nothing else. She didn't want to be like him and had always turned around when she reached M-28—the same highway the man had died along. But now that wasn't an option. She needed to be warm and safe, to be full in front of the TV with Emily, maybe reading her a book.

Another vehicle roared from behind her and she turned and stuck her thumb out. She couldn't recognize the driver; it was a dented black pickup and it too kept going. She wiped sleet from her face and stumbled past more house trailers. She had been at the yellow one a week ago to get high. The yard was covered with scrap lumber and twisted metal. An engine held by chains hung from a tree above a Pontiac with bleeding craters all over its body. If she gave up and went back maybe they could get more meth, think of another plan to bring Emily home.

The truck from earlier had turned around. It pulled off on the opposite side of the road. A man rolled down the window. "Hey, where you headed?"

"Munising," she said, "where you?"

"That way," he said. His left arm hung from the window, the elbow of his jacket ripped out, and he waved her over.

Amelia checked both ways and hurried across. She fingered the pipe in her pocket as she got closer to the truck. The Lake Superior wind ate through the trees and into the holes of her jeans, burning the flesh, and she buried her chin into the opening of her jacket.

"Are you sure it ain't no problem?"

"I don't guess so," he said, looking her over. "I could use company."

Amelia climbed into the cab. She put the bag on her lap and rested her feet on a toolbox on the floor. The truck smelled of sour milk and whiskey, causing an itch in her leaky nose. The man grabbed a stained pop bottle from a cup holder and spit into it. Then he worked his tongue into his cheek.

"So why you out hitching in this?" he asked.

"I ain't got much choice really, trying to get home."

"Well, you ought to be careful," he said, and lifted a hand toward the windshield. "This isn't the time of year you want to find yourself stranded."

She nodded and didn't say anything. She only wanted to get over to her mother's, take a hot shower and try to eat, wait for Emily to get home. She leaned her head against the window, exhaled, and fogged the glass, blurring bare patches of snow that swelled like blisters along the roadside.

"You drink?" He pulled a half bottle of Canadian whiskey from under the seat. "Here swallow the head on that, it'll warm you up, take the edge off," he said, and winked.

"No, I better not," she said. "I have some things to do later." She knew that she probably shouldn't show up high again, announcing that she had quit. Not to mention every time she drank, something bad happened.

"Go on, have a little taste, it won't hurt you none," he said, still holding the bottle out to her.

She decided one drink wouldn't hurt, and the man was probably right that it would warm her up, so she grabbed the bottle from his hand. She took a long swallow and shook and handed it back. "I ain't much for drinking," she said, grimacing and wiping her chin.

"No?" he said, giving her a doubtful look. "You seem like you've partied."

"Well maybe, but I wasn't much of a drinker."

She was still cold and her fingers hurt. She flexed them and tried not to lick at the blister on her lip. She wasn't sure the last time she ate something, so she hummed along to the roar of the engine to take her mind off that while her stomach burned. What would she tell her mother this time? Would she be supportive and allow her to stay or kick her out again? Last time her mother locked her out after she and Michael took off for a few days. Now, though, she'd only leave the house with her mother and Emily, show them that she was serious this time, mature enough to find a job, a place, the things needed to take care of Emily. Maybe for once she'd prove that she'd no longer be led by somebody else's actions.

When they reached Au Train, the snow began to fall more heavily; it blew in gusts off Superior and covered the dunes along both sides of the highway. A thin film of ice formed around the outer edges of the windshield, and the man held the empty bottle into the air and asked how the whiskey tasted. She only shrugged as he pulled off the highway toward a gas station. While he was in Bob's Booze Mart and she waited in the truck, a woman and a little girl walked across the parking lot, each carrying a plastic sack full of empties. The mother held the child's hand and jerked her along. The little girl never took her eyes off Amelia, even when a can slipped from her bag and was blown across the lot. The disgusted frown on the girl's face matched Emily's when Amelia's mother took her away.

After the woman and the girl disappeared into the store, Amelia fished the pipe out of her pocket and lowered herself in the seat. A man with a bowling ball stitched on the back of his green bomber jacket pumped gas. She flicked the lighter and sucked on the pipe, blew a cloud of meth smoke toward the windshield. Through the haze she watched as the truck driver came out holding a jug of whiskey. She slipped the pipe into her pocket as he got in the truck.

"We're going to take the scenic route, come into town the back way," he said. "It won't take any longer, and it will give us time to have more drinks."

Amelia nodded.

"Why does it smell like rotten eggs in here?" he asked.

Amelia rocked back and forth on the seat. She reached over and gripped the door handle. Her stomach had been in knots for weeks, twisted and stuck like a rusty chain. Now, though, the pain went numb, and she started to sweat. He grabbed a hold of the gearshift, dropped it down, and swung onto a seasonal road, forcing her to slide around on the seat.

"I'm surprised," she said, "there's people watching." She rubbed the frost from the passenger-side window with the sleeve of her jacket.

"People?" he asked, and looked out the window.

"The shadows. When they follow they never seem to stop."

The man shook his head as the truck slipped into a rut and fishtailed. He sat up on the wheel and guided the truck out of it. Every time they hit a bump, tools struck the lid of the tool box and sent vibrations through her body. The man lifted the bottle. He handed it to Amelia. She took a pull and winced and went back to studying the trees. She couldn't recall ever giving them much thought, how they seemed so skinny in the winter when their leaves fell off, how bare and helpless and alone they were against the cold.

"So you got a boyfriend or some family over here?"

"Yeah," she said, thinking nothing of it.

"He the one that did that to your face?"

She let out a little giggle and yanked on frayed strings around a hole in her jeans. She stuck the strings in her mouth and chewed on them. "Really, he's all I could ever want."

"What happened then? Seems someone took one of those car lighters to your face?"

She pulled a hand from her pocket and touched the front of her neck, stretching a piece of flesh with her thumb and index finger. "A rash."

"Uh huh," he said. "Looks like the same sores those folks got on the TV now."

Amelia leaned her head back and stared at the ceiling. She closed her eyes as he took snorts from the bottle, listened as mud slung from the tires and slapped the bottom of the truck. She had to pee. She stuck a hand in her jacket and applied pressure to her abdomen, thought about another hit, before moving on to thoughts of Emily instead. A few minutes later he stopped the truck in the middle of the road and killed the engine.

"Well," he said. "I best relieve myself." He turned and smiled, placing an arm along the top of the seat. "What about you?"

"I thought we were home?" She turned and looked out the front and back. Only the road cut between trees; the snow continued to fall. "I don't see my home here."

"We'll be in Munising soon enough," he said. "I only need to take a break. Maybe you shouldn't have any more whiskey."

The man got out of the truck. He walked to the back of it to block her sight, and placed a hand on the truck box. He started to pee. It echoed like water pouring from a rain gutter. She pulled the pipe out again and moved it in and out of the flame until the head of it blackened. Her lungs burned as they filled with smoke.

"What in Pete's hell?" He reached over and tried to grab the pipe from her hand.

"Don't touch me," she said, "not this time." Amelia wedged herself into the corner of the truck and stared at him. She still grasped the pipe in her right hand.

On a few occasions, after a four or five day high, when she and Michael had nothing to sell to continue the high, Michael had proposed that she help out. "Just do whatever the dealer wants," Michael had said. "You don't have to let yourself feel anything." She knew now there was no such thing as not feeling anything. Every time that she had undressed in front of a stranger and forced herself onto a bed, some act or smell had changed everything: how a man grunted in her ear, how his sheets could smell like bourbon and sweat that pinched her nose and clung to her skin afterward, how a man always gave a conquering smile as he lifted himself off of her. Now, she wasn't about to let this man have his way with her, too.

"Please," she said. "I wasn't looking for sex when I got in for a ride. I got a daughter."

"What in the hell are you talking about?"

He grabbed a hold of the steering wheel and pulled himself into the truck. He looked through the windshield. Small chunks of snow fell onto the hood and melted as if it were hitting a hot spoon. "You know," he said, facing straight ahead, "somebody needs to help you."

"No," she said. "I never said you could have me." She felt she had to do something to take his mind off her, but she was too buzzed to think of anything. So she reached over and turned the truck key. "Friends," she said, and started the truck. "We wouldn't be after the other way."

"You," he said, "ought to be let out at the hospital. If you have a daughter you shouldn't let her see you like this."

"Please, don't do that."

"Don't what?" he asked, and ran a hand through his hair.

"Touch me down there."

The man groaned and turned his head toward the driver's side window. She wondered what might happen if she grabbed a wrench off the floorboard and knocked him over the head with it, would that work? Would he decide not to touch her then? She didn't think so.

"Listen," he said, and placed a hand on her shoulder and squeezed. "I'm not going to touch you. The faster you get your footing the sooner you go home, a win-win," and he removed his hand.

When he let go, she imagined him trying to pinch the flesh around her spine as he slid her over the seat and forced her head down onto him.

"God, no," she said. "I'll bite."

He said, "You need to get your shit together and quit spinning out. I ain't going to jail." He tried to grab a hold of her, shake her out of the madness, but she resisted.

"Come on," he said. "Don't make me do something I'll regret. Now give me the drugs."

Before she could make another plea and shove his hands away, a burning splash of liquid shot from her mouth and coated the truck's dash. He let out a yell and tried to get her door open, tried to nudge her out. He looked at the fluid leaking into the heater vent and pinned her against the passenger-side door with a free hand. She kicked at him. She got her fingers around the door handle and fell out onto her back. He thrashed inside the cab and the truck lurched. He threw open his door, then rounded the rear of the truck.

"Goddamn it," he said, "come here."

Amelia got to her feet. She grabbed the plastic bag and ran into the woods. At first he seemed to be right behind her and she tripped over a fallen tree.

"Girl," he said, bent over with his head up halfway down the hill. "I'm sorry. Come get in the truck and I'll take you home. I want to help."

The bag Amelia carried ripped during the fall. She gathered the clothes from the hillside and crammed them in as best she could. Down toward the road the man yelled again. Her lungs burned, along with her elbow and knee. She could always turn around and give herself to the man, do whatever it took, like Michael would have urged, to get what she wanted, but she opted to keep going. After jumping a creek and crossing a few small ridges, her legs became tired and she couldn't tell which direction she had come. At the bottom of a ravine she found an uprooted hemlock and crawled underneath it, to shield the wind and snow. She could hear the faint rumble of the truck echoing through the hills, its horn, and she shivered, hugged the bag. Through a tangle of roots she watched as the dense pine bog slowly succumbed to snow. She leaned her head back and the earth spun—felt the wetness burn down her thighs—and remembered being a child and pulling a doll with a cord around its neck in the summer sun when she heard Emily laugh. She tried to lift her head and call out, but the night sky had already covered her with a blanket of darkness.

Politician's Logic

If Obama is related to president Bush,
I am a genius of classroom politics,
The opposite of a dumb tree.
Because money swims in a wealthy man's pocket,
You are no glorified suit.

If Hitler was Jewish,
I am a slave to the white aristocracy,
The opposite of a rich tobacco owner.
Because green sprouts from the trees of tax payers,
You are a jobless man hanging by a thread.

If the White House could talk,
I am a chimp that does sign language,
The opposite of a fish with wings.
Because lies, promises, and speeches are a one-way road,
You are the king, president, and a dirty little sock,
no one can find.

If the moon was a politician,
I am the sun of a nation,
The opposite of a knight saving his princess.
Because no earth can hold your weight,
You are the single most hated man
with the power of a baby.

If you were a white collared snake,
I am a blue collared car,
The opposite of a catholic priest at mass.
Because having this position means freedom,
You are a slithering, sweet talking mouth that burns
holes into other people's ideas.

Crocodile

Crocodile perched on the couch. He watched her pace the apartment.

She looked at her watch. She paused at the mirror and tossed her hair, put red lipstick on, adjusted her necklace.

"Do you know where my phone is?" she asked Crocodile.

He didn't know what to say. Or if to say anything. He sat.

She sat on the couch next to him and shoved her hands into the corners, under the cushions, under the pillows. She smacked her hand into the burgundy fabric.

"Shoot," she said.

He wanted to open his mouth. Bite her. Bite her hand. But he couldn't. He sometimes looked at the birds on the fire escape and envied them. Their little beaks opening and closing, making calls, carrying bits of string or pieces of bagel. He'd strain to open his mouth, part his jaws, but he was sewn together so tightly.

She stared into the mirror again. He watched as she shrugged her shoulders, tossed her hair again, then raked her fingers through it. Always, she was like this. Always, she stood at the mirror. He wished he could look into a mirror. He had no idea what he looked like. He feared what he looked like.

Crocodile imagined a stuffed animal won at a carnival. Acrylic fabric. Lime green. Google eyes. He wished, hoped, this wasn't true. He hoped he looked even a little tough, even a little like a crocodile.

She sat next to him again. "I can't find my fucking phone," she said. She sat back, looked at her watch, said, "Shit," and then left. The locks clanked into place, each one, down the door like a cracking spinal cord.

He wriggled. He squirmed.

He fell from the couch.

On his belly, he scooted to the fire escape, to the floor- to-ceiling window. He couldn't see the top of the window from directly beneath it. His lack of neck wouldn't allow it.

He shuffled and pushed his way under the sill. He saw the window across the way. He saw the street, long in both directions. There were birds. Little brown ones. There were potted flowers sitting on the escape. Little pink ones.

Crocodile paused. He savored the air. He wondered what things smelled like.

He fell. Down the fire escape, he fell. He had wanted this for so long. To feel the wind on his back, his belly, his long, scaly tail.

He landed with a thud on the pavement. He tried to look up to the window, but he could not. He thought of her. How she'd sit in fuzzy pants, he liked how soft they were, and eat popcorn and pat his head. Sometimes she spoke to him. Asked him questions. He felt sorry for her.

He hadn't realized the pavement was wet. His belly was damp and cold. It made him uncomfortable. Nothing like the soft couch. He wriggled. He squirmed. He wondered if she ever felt sorry for him. And would she feel sorry for him now?

What would he do? His belly was wet. He had no baking soda to rub away the grime. He began to scoot. He would look in a mirror. See himself. See Crocodile.

Growing Mad in Brooklyn

Torn and twisted in the torrent of the full moon night
pieces of my life, charged up with caffeine, floating in liquor
barefoot through the gutters of the mutant pyramid
we were made to believe in and climb
sacrificing every last holy scrap of being
in exchange for an irrelevant lottery ticket
the winner of which will get to cut
the last winner's throat!
and the crowds will cheer
zealously hungry for blood
that will sanctify their own surrender

Mad with southern winds of chance
swooping in with violent gusts
upon prophetic wings
of carelessly naked lovers
devout and sublime
in their acts of self inflicted torture
and burning pleasure
abandoning hallucinatory justifications
founded on zodiac rhymes and riddles
pronounced by drunk demigods
perverted by the illusions of our fathers

Seeking patience in the midst
of the full-fledged panic rage
that like the mist, exudes
from the concrete pores

of the summer city
rank with rotting garbage
of mass-produced misery
rolling up the South Slope streets
with a swagger of the sunrise birds
sick in the gut with a spinning head
severally blown, fucked and broke

Falling Under the Rabbit

I don't think it's going to stop.

The three of them are on the front porch, legs curled under them on the sagging couch. They're drinking coffee as the rain splashes on the cactus plants in the front yard, more than a dash of whiskey stirred into the cracked cups in their hands.

What do you feel like doing?

Marianne leaves a smear of red lipstick around her coffee cup. She tells people she was named after Marianne Faithfull, and after a hard night her voice bears a resemblance. Bonnie's name means 'pretty one', which never fails to make her blush when someone teases her about it.

Bonnie shrugs. *I don't want to go out in that. Do you?*

Marianne and Kat shake their heads at the same time.

We could watch Japanese horror movies all afternoon.

We could bake a salted caramel pudding and eat the entire thing.

We could frock up and dance to Betty Davis in high heels on the lounge room floorboards.

Bonnie's so focused on the drops hitting the soil that at first she's not sure which one of them suggests it. The rain is making her head hurt.

We could build a pillow fort.

The frown shoots across her face before she can stop it.

A what?

Marianne turns to her and taps her thigh with a purple nail.

You know Bon-Bon, when you were a kid? When it rained and you weren't allowed outside, didn't you ever build a pillow fort, with blankets and pillows and chairs? And you curled up inside, all hidden and cosy, and pretended no-one could ever find you?

Bonnie doesn't move. The only safe place she remembers from childhood was under her bed, until he started looking for her there too.

Kat's laughing, and in one swift movement is on her feet.

Let's do it! Come on girls, crank up the funk and get building.

The three of them head for the front bedroom. There's a huge painting of a rabbit on the moss green wall above the bed. Marianne and Kat scoop the blankets into their arms, instinct guiding their movements.

Bonnie waits by the door.

Kat throws her a pillow, almost smacking her in the face.

Hey babe, jump in. You know what to do.

Bonnie doesn't move.

Bonnie doesn't know what to do.

The rabbit is watching her with its wide brown eyes.

Marianne hefts a straight backed chair onto the bed, humming to the music. Bonnie is watching her friends as her heart starts to tap against her rib cage and the words inside her head start to stretch their arms, and slowly wake up.

You'll fuck this up.

They're shimmying as they throw another chair onto the mattress, heads bent in laughter as the bass line thumps.

You can't build a shelter. You can't build somewhere safe for your friends.

The rabbit doesn't blink.

You can't keep your friends safe. What if you put a pillow in the wrong place and you all climb inside and you can't get out? What if at that moment the world stops still and you're all inside and you've built it all wrong, you're going to build it wrong and you'll all have to live there forever and they'll never be safe again.

Did the rabbit just nod?

Bonnie's palms are beginning to tingle.

It's never safe.

No-one knows that more than you.

Kat looks up. She pauses, and holds out a hand to get Marianne's attention. The two girls aren't dancing now. The look on Bonnie's face is the same as when they'd found her on the roof that day, talking to the swallows in the liquid amber tree. Kat slides her hand into Marianne's as they stand there, watching their friend with wary eyes and heavy hearts.

Marianne is the first to move.

Babe, why don't you add a pillow? Put it anywhere you like.

Bonnie's gaze moves down slowly from the painting to her friend.

Once we're inside, nothing can touch us.

Bonnie reaches for the pillow.

She walks towards the fort, blankets draped over chairs on top of the mattress. While she's been watching the rabbit, Marianne has placed books inside, and leaned the bottle of whiskey against them. There are yellow tulips too, with their petals only just beginning to curl, the faintest tinge of brown staining their edges.

It does look cosy, she thinks. *It looks cosy, and warm, with the rain still beating against the window.*

But it could be a trap, the rabbit whispers, so quietly she's sure the other two haven't heard.

She stands beside the bed and lifts the pillow. She holds it over the mattress and hesitates, keeps her eyes closed for a long moment. When she opens them, she places the pillow inside the fort with one quick movement, and then jumps back.

She stands under the rabbit's gaze, and waits for it all to collapse.

The Stalk and Beads

1

My brother James' son has a tall corn stalk in his right hand as a staff shepherding through the neighborhood naked and crying and casting off 'devils' with his left hand, with the rosary beads I bought him last week for his eighteenth birthday. The Turtles are watching him intently, other than eyes their helmeted kid heads barely visible behind the long barrier, each kid thinking this could be the day he's finally called to duty.

2

To their training, for these kids, he's a pattern now. It wasn't more than two weeks ago when he stripped off again and heaved his shirt up over the barbed wire at Glenfada and heaved himself up with it, deliberately caught in the menace. The Brits wanted to shoot; they all have hairs on their shoulders and standing orders there behind the wall. But Father D'Arcy got there quick and I came running too and together we calmed them. "Liberties," said the Father. "He's just testing his liberties. He's no trouble to you." Even still, one of them fired a warning so loud it startled the boy to the ground, his chest all sliced up and bloody meat from the razor barbs, the orange and white of his flag tattoo tattered and bright red.

3

In the wet chill, I'm running after him. "Brendan You Fuck," I say out of breath when I near him. He doesn't respond, doesn't even turn around, like he's deaf or dumb.

4

I've been telling James the boy needs help. He's ill in some way that none of us know. But James is just obstinate and leaves him there for days in that carved out rubble fall near Fahan they call an apartment. I told him too they should have moved after the boy's mother left, their seventeen years quicked in a five word note: 'Gone to a whiskeyless house.' She seemed to carry around some feeling of nostalgia for what she had imagined her life here with James was supposed to be but never was. Little Brendan took one hard that night and every night after it, I'd imagine: James likes to tell me his ideas about tenderizing kids for the grill like rough steak.

5

From ten meters away, if Brendan were to shout 'Go home' or 'Brits out' the Squaddies would probably know just to leave him pass. They've trained for that. But he instead shouts some long incomprehensible string of half words and ends crazily in a verse on "all men are endowed by their creator" and "all men are subject to one another" and so three of the kids shoot him. He falls the way all shot children fall. And I can see smoke rising from behind the wall and steam rising from Brendan's chest and the streams of white wrapping together against the gray like through a funnel til they become indistinct against the clouds that always blanket this part of the sky. And the reports echo madly, rattle around all the cement buildings and barricades and alcoves and doorways along the road and I can tell the type of weapon by the time the reverberations take to reach me and once they're done and the Brits are away to safety with their rucks I go to Brendan through the rubble and kneel at his side where the stalk and beads have gathered neatly and his neatly scabbed and pocked chest is cold now and I can see that he's already passed and the situation's done. This is precisely why though James insists they sound more like claps of thunder I've always thought of the reports as slamming doors.

6

I've no strength to carry him off and so I move the stalk to cover him and leave him there in the street and go down to the Free Corner to find Father D'Arcy, who's out for the day, I'm told. Streets away now, I think about walking back toward the wall but don't really care to see the body, spirit escaped, or risk the short-haired Toms that shot him. Too, I stop into Murph's and he's already set up a pint by the time I get the words out and so I stay. I figure that somebody from the City's already come to collect him or at least is probably on his way and he's probably trained better than I am how to handle these types of things.

Inventing the Wheel

The problem was, the dang long johns kept getting bunched up at her knees inside her very tight jeans, and when they did that she really couldn't pull them up all the way, so it's like she was wearing her pants low around her ass like Li'l Wayne or someone, which would maybe have been okay if it was Halloween or if she was twenty, but she wasn't. The bunching was uncomfortable, and it was cold outside, too cold to wear thick tights underneath her jeans. Thick tights wouldn't deaden the sting of a windy negative ten degrees. That kind of cold that called for old fashioned long underwear that bunched and made you miserable. She needed to wear the kind of long johns don't really fit under any jeans that actually fit your body, which happened to be the only kind of jeans that Taylor owned. She liked skinny jeans, fitted right up to the slim curve of her ankles, which were too slim, really for any kind of skinny jean to accommodate. A foot couldn't fit through any opening as small as Taylor's ankles. They were a point of pride, and in spring, summer, even through most of fall she walked around with them on display. In winter, their feminine delicacy was a hindrance. No boots that fit her at the ankles could accommodate the way her jeans bunched around them. She would not wear wider boots. She refused to let people believe she had cankles. Her pants had to be cuffed at the top of her boots. It was drafty, but more comfortable than the deep red divots the pressure of the denim seams left in her skin. Those indents wouldn't leave until morning, really, at which point she needed to put the jeans back on again, over tights to make winter in Minnesota less painful. So the jeans were always cuffed. Much of the draft could be eliminated by wearing thick wool socks pulled up as high as they'd go. That was the usual strategy, and she could barely remember a time that she'd needed the waffle-knit long underwear her Mom had given her three Christmases ago when she'd first moved away from home. The high temperature for the day was negative fifteen degrees and windy, and Taylor didn't have a car anymore, so she was being very brave for even thinking about going outside. That's what she kept telling herself.

Taylor took the jeans off and flipped them inside out. She pulled the long johns down over her heels and stepped on them to keep them in place. Very slowly she tried to reverse engineer the act of taking pants off. She put the jean's inside out cuffs around her ankles, and very slowly tried to peel them on. The only way to even try it seemed to be lying on the bed, flat on her back with her legs in the air like gravity would put the pants on for her. Of course the plan was doomed from the very beginning. The more time she spent trying to move slowly, the more tangled up she got. It took more time than it needed to for her to give up and put her jeans right side out. Next, she put them on right side out but only so far up as her ankles. Waddling to the junk drawer, she fished out a pair of nose-needle pliers, reached up the ankle of her pant leg to get a grip on the hem of the long johns and pulled. Figuring if she could prevent the bunching from happening in small increments, that the bunching itself would be more generally stopped, she focused. She gripped the pliers. She yanked. She pulled her pants up just a little higher. She gripped the pliers. She yanked. She pulled her pants up a little higher. That's right, she murmured to herself. Slow and steady. Slow and steady wins the race. There's a reason Mama always said so.

Like maybe that your mama's not any good at doing things fast? Brian was propped up against the door frame with his arms crossed looking gangly as ever and pleased with himself for not being the asshole on the floor with the tools shoved up his pants. He always sort of loved when he caught Taylor in positions like this. At parties he liked to tell all their friends the story of the night he came home to find her fixing a doorknob with a butter knife. He liked to feel superior. Maybe he was superior. Either way, he was her boyfriend, and even if he wasn't the asshole on the floor with needle-nose pliers up his pants, he was the asshole right then. Taylor felt it.

Shut up. It's cold out. They keep bunching.

You know, if you just tuck them into your socks, it'll be the same as when you wear tights. The elastic from the socks holds them in place, see?

Oh, Taylor said. It was all she could manage to say without seeming to feel. It meant oh, I didn't realize before. Oh, you're in a mood again. Oh, I think I did it that way once before. Oh, I didn't know you'd be like this when I promised you I'd love you forever. Oh, oh, oh. Oh my.

Jesus Christ, you'd think you'd never gotten dressed before.

I haven't had any coffee yet.

Do you want me to make you some?

Yes, please.

Brian put the coffee in a thermos without being asked and tied the chin strap of her fur lined hat before she went out the door, being sweet because he knew he usually wasn't. He kissed her on her forehead, and told her to keep her face covered up with a scarf. Being loved by Brian sometimes made Taylor feel small. He kissed her on the forehead as often as he kissed her properly. Ever since winter came, she found herself remembering the tall, skinny boy from before with unkempt hair had crooked teeth. He was sunshine. There was light behind his eyes, behind his skin, and before she ever thought of loving him, she'd told him everything she never realized she'd never told anyone before.

His first kiss was a lunge. That was something worth remembering. They'd been together on a blanket on the grass of the quad with their books, not studying. They were just kids. Spring was a time for learning, but not for books, he'd said. It seemed like such a wise thing to say, and he was standing above her pacing and kicking at rocks in the grass, dribbling one rock back and forth between his feet like a flattened soccer ball. She leaned back on her elbows and told him about leaving home, about how she always felt so bumbling and uncomfortable. She told him she'd carried around index cards of advice she'd written to herself, and that she'd shuffle them and read through them again out of order, like vocabulary flash cards from grammar school. DON'T BE A FREAK. RELAX SO PEOPLE WILL THINK

YOU ARE RELAXED. SMILE SO PEOPLE WILL KNOW YOU WANT TO BE THEIR FRIEND. He came at her in a burst with his whole body, knocking her over and underneath him, their teeth clinking together. He squeezed her tight. My god, he shouted to the sky, it's like you're inventing the goddamn wheel. He had just discovered blasphemy. Raised Lutheran, and in his first months away from home he loved the power that comes with daring God and everyone to strike him down. Inventing the wheel, he'd said. You know, I could really learn to love you for a very long time. Right after their very first kiss, he'd said it. Probably, if you asked him, he'd say it now. Taylor hadn't thought of him for a very long time.

The cold gave her a headache that stuck her behind the eyes every time she took a step, and at the bus stop she swayed along with the wind to keep from freezing right into place. It was still dark, even though it was morning, and the traffic was thick, and all the lights twinkled together to look like the sign of an approaching bus. She waited five minutes, and when it came the door opened and heat burst out at her like she was who it had been looking for all this time. She sat down, closed her eyes, worked at sleeping without sleeping so much that she didn't hear the driver call the stops. The bus was almost always quiet in the mornings, but this morning the Mexican man with dreadlocks, Ruben, boarded with his fat friend whose name Taylor had never heard. She liked them together. Apart, they were just odd. Together, they were a perfect fit.

We're having a celebration after work today, Ruben said to his fat friend.

What for?

It's my supervisor's three year anniversary with the company. The good kind of party, nothing fancy. We're just going to play some good music out by the loading dock, drink a little bit. You should come by. Lots of people will be there.

Yeah?

Yeah, man. And check this out what I got him. Manischewitz. It's Jewish. This is the blackberry kind. Cheap, too, but you wouldn't know it.

Oh, I know that stuff. I remember, me and my dad used to sit out by the train tracks at night when the weather was good. That was his drink. Not for any normal day, that was his special occasion drink that he saved for when the weather was nice.

Well then it's fate, isn't it? You've got to come. We can drink blackberry manischewitz, and pretend the it's not so cold out that our balls are trying to crawl all the way inside. Hey, we'll even have a toast to your father and everything.

Maneschewitz. It was a drink Taylor drank when she was first learning what it was to be drunk. At the time, she hated how it made her lips stained purple. Hearing of it from Ruben she knew that if she ever tried it again, she wouldn't mind at all.

Can I come?

The words were out, just hanging in the air before she knew she was going to say them. Ruben, who she knew but who didn't know her, stopped short. He just looked at her, considering.

I'm sorry. I didn't mean. I don't. She kept her eyes trained on her gloved hands. She spoke quietly. I'm not, she said. I remember manischewitz.

It was all happening so fast. Everything she'd learned before, she needed to learn again. ACT LIKE EVERYONE AROUND YOU HAS KNOWN YOU FOR YEARS ALREADY. It used to work, but it didn't anymore. It didn't work the same way nothing old ever worked after awhile.

I know you, Ruben said. He said it like a question, and kept his eyes on her, head back, squinting but not unfriendly.

Sort of, Taylor said. Not really, I guess. We ride the bus together sometimes.

Okay, Ruben said. Yeah, sure.

He even looked like he meant it. Suspicious, but happy.

I'll bring something, she said.

Oh, that's cool, Ruben said. That's really cool of you to do that.

Taylor's phone rang, and she knew it was Brian. Nobody else would call so early in the day, so she let it ring. Thanks, she said. It sounds like a really fun time.

Yeah, Ruben said. I think it will be.

The phone chimed, and she had a text from Brian. You forgot your lunch. I'll drop it off later. I love you anyways. Promise. :D How it was possible to love then hate then love again in such quick succession, Taylor could never understand. But everything she'd ever learned someone else had told her first, and she'd then learned for herself years later, and then again years later after that when time had made the first learning of it had become stale and forgettable. Like love. Like living at all. Some days it was like she'd never gotten dressed before. Some days, it occurred to her again for the very first time that didn't have to be a bad thing, living that way.

Next stop Light Rail, the driver called out. Be careful getting out, it's all ice down there, he warned her. Stepping out into the cold her face froze again and tingled, and before she pulled her scarf up above her mouth and nose, she inhaled a big breath that made her lungs ache and blew out a giant puff of frozen smoke that curled up into the wind in a way that made her move inside her coat.

Slow Song

There are no airplanes today in the sky of New York. I guess
they sleep beneath the fresh snow. And maybe, just occasionally
from under the white covered fuselage appears a small glimmer,
as if they wink at the people to tell them that they know the game.
I guess that the pilots are somewhere warm, waiting for the snow
to stop, waiting for their flight attendants to smile. So it goes like
that in heaven. Or maybe I'm wrong? Here on earth the whiskey is
perfect. Naturally with rocks, although that is somewhat stupid. I am
known for living awful, when life is good. I have no money to build
a chapel, but I light a candle, which ignites the icy diamonds in my
glass and I walk towards the edge, I can hear the edge calling me
quietly. It starts snowing again. The planes have the nightmares of all
their fallen brothers. But now I'm here and I look out the window.
The fresh snow falls deep and covers the phone wire along with two
nestled pigeons. I am waiting for the call that will shake them off, back
to life.

River Road Redemption

Ray Cutter was an optimist but he hated to be positive. Ray took a small breath and held it, dammed up in a reservoir behind his pursed lips. Pinching one of the dark window curtains between his thumb and index finger Ray pulled it cautiously to one side. When the Oxy runs out his hands shake, so he pulled the curtain as cautiously as he could under the circumstances.

Ancient grease and dirt slurped from the curtain-fabric and stuck to his jerky fingers as he pulled the curtain back. Ray didn't like to open the curtains, not even a sliver, or the windows or the doors. But, he did it anyway because he had no choice when the pressure in the house, but especially when the pressure in Ray's hands became too great. Sometimes, that pressure in his hands became so great that Ray just had to bleed a little off, by opening a curtain, a window, maybe a door.

Ray never trusted it, the outside that is, since it was always subject to change, subject to interpretation, there were no certainties outside. Inside, the world inside was controlled, certain and he controlled the horizontal, he controlled the vertical. Ray pushed his blinking, twitchy right eye into the crack, into the sliver of light from the outside which knifed into the room, admitted between the curtains. Watching. Looking.

"Looks methy out there," Ray thought. Just the way he wanted it. The look which keeps the judging eyes away. Ray had been waiting for them, expecting their arrival in his gravel driveway at any moment. They would come, Ray was sure of it and he would be ready. Just a gate keeper, pressure on, pressure off, on-off.

The trampoline was still in the same place undisturbed in the front yard. Ray Junior stopped using it last summer after he jammed the hell out of his fingers jumping on that thing. That was the day eight-year-old Ray Junior got religion, or rather Ray Cutter's hands gave Ray Junior religion. Ray's hands told him to do it, and so the first two fingers of his right hand dipped into the Ovaltine and baptized Ray Junior on the forehead in the name of the Father, the Son and the Holy Ghost, Amen. A few sticky clumps of the partially undissolved baptismal Ovaltine mud stuck to little Ray's eyebrows. After that, they called him "Baptized Ray."

A layer of green moss covered the black trampoline fabric, no one had disturbed the green film. The two rusted camper tops remained where he threw them several years ago in his front yard except for tall grass leaning sideways under the weight of a heavy morning dew, growing through the broken plastic windows and the rusted out holes in the camper tops. But he didn't own a pickup truck. Ray hated pickup trucks, he hated people who drove pickup trucks. No one had moved these either, all undisturbed.

Through the curtain-slit he could see the door to his large rusting metal windowless shed on his side yard. The chain and lock were still in place. There was no evidence, none that he could see anyway in the curtain-slit that anything had changed, or that anyone had tampered with the shed or the lock on the shed.

Through the curtain-slit he could see the decaying ruin of the old wooden barn which leaned precariously to the side. Planks on the barn were rotted and falling away so that westerly breezes passed through the structure unimpeded. The ancient roof bowed excessively under the weight of thick green moss which covered the rotted cedar shakes. No one had disturbed the leaning barn and it was just as it had always been for decades: undisturbed and on the verge of sudden, catastrophic collapse under the hulking weight of its own history. There would be time to take care of that also, later. Ray hated people who followed up on follow-up details.

For now, Ray Cutter was by the window, hand on the curtain, hand at the door, waiting for them to arrive. He looked down at the baseball bat that he kept in the tall wicker basket by the front door to stop intruders. If they wanted to bring this on, then fine with Ray. Ray's hands seemed to twitch toward the bat but Ray wasn't sure if he interpreted this right.

Ray's house, his rental house, was on River Road which was a mossy and wet two-lane country strip of pot-holed asphalt with deep runoff ditches along the sides. River Road ran through muddy and foggy cow pastures within a hundred yards of the Columbia River outside Clatskanie, Oregon. It was a wet, damp, swampy crease in the hills along a thin strip of flatlands along the river. The sun does not shine often and the moss is thick in Clatskanie. Everything is damp and wet most of the year. The property had been a farm years ago, long before Ray arrived with Marcie and Baptized Ray. But, Ray had no cows, Ray was no farmer, Ray hated farms, he hated farmers.

Ray was a writer, but he hated to write. Ray hated writers. "I write with my hands, not my brain. Writing is a compulsion. I write because I have to, there's no choice. It's like it's dictated to me and I am compelled to write," is what Ray told his mother when she would listen, or he'd tell to Marcie his wife or the four previous wives which held Ray's hands in marriage when they would listen.

His mother, his wives, they always listened at the start, but then they drifted away and lost focus. Ray knew that they rolled their eyes when he talked about writing. Ray knew they turned their faces to the side so he could not see them. But, Ray did not have the luxury of looking away, of ignoring what his hands were compelled to write, when they were so compelled. They can turn away, they might snicker, Ray thought, but Ray knew that he had no choice with his hands, he couldn't turn away.

The thing was that Ray's hands had not written in more than 18 months. Even when his hands did write there was little money in it. Certainly not enough money for Marcie, Baptized Ray and him to live on. Ray could feel the pressure to write building in his hands. Soon. He would be writing soon.

While Ray's hands lay in hibernation waiting for sufficient pressure to awaken them, each and every month checks made their way up from Shirley in Portland, to Ray's landlord in Astoria, to pay his rent. Shirley

Cutter, Ray's mother, held her 42 year old son in a tight but chilled embrace, more like a queen bee cool-ly holding her thousands of children than mother. In a cemetery in Parkland, Oregon, there was an unoccupied cemetery plot waiting with a headstone with Ray's name and date of birth carved into the stone ready for him. All that was needed was to carve in the date of Ray's death and to insert his body, of course, into the ground. Right there beside his twin sister, Ellie, who died at 6 weeks after their birth.

Ray never knew Ellie, his deceased twin sister, in any traditional sense since she died when he was only 6 weeks old. But, Ellie always loomed next to him and with him and over him. When his mother thought of Ray she thought of Ellie. For Ray's mother, there was no separation between them even 42 years later after their birth-death. Ray's mother blamed Ray and Ray blamed himself, for taking the mother's milk that caused his twin to die.

So, the checks came up from Ray's mother in Portland every month to Ray's landlord's dry and modern post office box in a prim office park in Astoria were the money was swept and bundled with other rent checks into pristine wire transfers for absentee landlords in Seattle. And his cemetery plot and his head stone waited for Ray, beside deceased 6 week old Ellie, who Ray never spoke to but who was always there beside him, waiting for him, judging him.

Pressure was building, always building under the weighty glare of Ellie's eyes, Ellie's judgment. Ellie wanted to know, Ray's mother wanted to know, what Ray was doing with the life that he took from Ellie, the life of the daughter that Ray took from his mother. The rent checks kept coming every month, and in summer the cemetery plot in Parkland was being mowed and trimmed around his headstone always ready for him. Meanwhile, Ray was in his house in Clatskanie, peeking out the window through the greasy curtain-slit, over his methy yard. Ray was ready.

It was a small and mossy wood-framed house on River Road where Ray lived with Marcie, his fifth wife, and Baptized Ray. Ray was a husband, five times over, but he hated to husband. The house was just over 700 square foot for the three of them but it still felt like too much space for Ray. Small houses, confined spaces, that's what Ray wanted. Ray liked to live in small houses and his mother liked the lower rents.

In a small house with only a few walls tightly restraining him, Ray felt that he had better control of letting the pressure off or keeping it building. There was one thing that Ray knew about his life and that was that this small house, his rusting shed, the leaning barn, the moldy, slimy trampoline, Marcie and Baptized Ray and above all else twin sister Ellie, his mother and his writing were all part of the pressurized System of Ray. Separately the parts were just a collection of random people and things and vain hopes of little significance. But, once you tighten the bolts down on the whole group together into a pressurized system, once Ray tied them to their common shared meaning then that's a whole other thing and each part of the system adds and subtracts pressure from the whole. Pressure is about control, control is about pressure. These are one and the same things.

It didn't matter where Ray was or what he was doing, it was always a pressurized system on the verge with all ten toes hanging out over the edge almost twisting wildly out of control. Ray hated the pressure but he couldn't escape it, he managed it as best he could. More about that later.

Watching the doors and windows waiting for the outside world, the police, the FBI, the IRS, the government men, DB Cooper, or the prior wives (there were always the pissed off prior wives, like more lost twins, more judging eyes) to come around and arrest him or interrogate him. But he had his proof that it wasn't just in his mind. There was the break-in, the friggin break-in. Ray, Marcie and Baptized Ray had been away, out of the house for just a few minutes 18 months ago. Ray didn't want to leave but he had to go to the doctor to renew his Oxycodone prescription. He was in pain, yes, that was it, intense back pain and the Oxy prescription had run out.

That's when the break-in happened. His safe, the one he kept in the crawl space under the floor of the bedroom he shared with Marcie, had been stolen. Whoever took it, they knew just where the safe was. They went right to it and they didn't take anything else, not even the guns on the floor under the bed. The safe, his manuscripts, his unpublished novels, cancelled checks. Everything in the safe was gone. The disappearance of the safe was devastating and Ray's hands stopped writing and had not written in the 18 months since the break-in. All Ray could do was laugh at the loss. He reported the crime to the police. But, the police did nothing, no one was ever arrested and nothing was ever recovered or found. Everything in the safe, all of Ray's work, was lost forever.

But Ray wasn't sure about the break-in. Maybe Ray's memory had failed, maybe Ray got it wrong about the break-in and there was no break-in at all. Ray could not be certain that he did not do it himself, maybe Ray had taken the safe himself and threw it into the Columbia River. Sometimes Ray did things like that under the Oxy and the booze and under the pressure of Ellie's eyes, under the weight of his mother's eyes, or when the pressure in his hands was too great. Ray couldn't be completely sure.

But, he was pretty sure that it was stolen and the authorities did nothing. He was under surveillance by the FBI, he was sure of it. They broke in to steal his manuscripts. Maybe they were on their way now to his house, maybe this was the day of the great, final conflagration of Ray. Today, this would be the day of Ray's Ruby Ridge, or Ray's Branch Davidian Waco incineration, or Ray's Jones Town, Guyana disaster. Maybe today was the final day to bleed off all the pressure in a great wasting. More about that later.

Marcie set all this in motion today, this morning. Two hours ago Marcie gathered up Baptized Ray, the car keys, the Chevy and nothing else. Ray remembered that there was something about how quickly Marcie walked around their house, there was a sudden but silent urgency in her movement. Marcie didn't say anything as she left the house, nothing about where she was going or when she would return. She left when Ray went to the bathroom, she propped a kitchen chair at a tilted angle against the doorknob, which only delayed Ray's exit from the bathroom.

There was that look of fear in Marcie's eyes and in Baptized Ray's eyes when they watched Ray this morning. Ray recognized the look now, in retrospect. "Rockin' Ray" she called him when he rocked on his heels. Ray stood in the middle of their small family room, with his fists wrapped in a white knuckle grip around the baseball bat. "So when is she gonna get here with the Oxy prescription? When?" Ray hated to wait for deliveries, especially when it was his Oxy. Ray hated delivery people.

Ray put one hand then the other hand in the back pockets of his jeans. Ray would tuck the baseball bat under his arm and then push his hands together, fist to palm, fist to palm, over and over again. And there was the rocking on his heels. "How long can it take her to get here?" Ray was rocking, always rocking back and forth on his heels, then pacing back and forth in the small TV room by the front door, curtains drawn, of course.

"Friggin' FBI" Ray said this morning just like he had said many mornings before. "Friggin breakin, I'll have to start my work all over again."

Thinking back on that moment this morning Ray remembered the look in Marcie's face as she looked at him. Baptized Ray stopped watching TV and looked at him also. When they looked into his face they could see that he was sweating, he weaved about the room with a dizziness, they tell his heart beat fiercely in his chest, he anxiously awaited the delivery.

Marcie didn't say it but he could hear her voice inside her head saying "Rockin Ray." Ray could see the way that Baptized Ray and Marcie looked at him, Ray had been divorced four times before and he knew the look. Within less than ten minutes after he saw that look in Marcie's and Baptized Ray's faces, just as soon as Ray went in the bathroom to take a dump, Marcie grabbed Baptized Ray and they were gone. That was two hours ago.

As soon as Ray left the bathroom he could tell immediately from the silence and the feel of his small house that they were gone and gone for good. And, for the last two hours Ray looked out through the curtain-slit. Waiting and looking. Marcie would be back for her stuff, he was sure. And, Marcie would bring her brother and the police this time, he was sure.

Then through the curtain-slit Ray saw a car come down River Road. It was an old Sunbird with rust and faded blue paint which pulled into his driveway and stopped. A young and attractive woman with long black hair got out of the car. She looked familiar but Ray did not know her. Maybe it was Ellie, his deceased twin. Ray's looking eye blinked quickly in the curtain-slit and his breathing accelerated. After all these years, has she come to see him? But, through the curtain-slit she looked too young to be his twin. Why would she have frozen at 20 years old and not aged further. Certainly this woman had not aged from the hard years that etched into Ray. He had the feeling that he liked her, but he didn't know why. She walked up the driveway toward their front door.

She knocked on the door and announced "Delivery. Delivery."

Ray opened the door and realized immediately that this woman was the delivery person from the pharmacy with his Oxy. This was not Ellie although she is what he imagined Ellie would look like if she were alive. Ray immediately took the bag from her hands which held his Oxy, reached in, opened the prescription bottle and took one of the capsules and put it in his mouth, then worked up his saliva to swallow it. The delivery woman remained at the door, holding a half-clip board out toward Ray.

"Mr. Cutter, I wish you wouldn't grab your prescription like that. Deliveries are just a convenience to certain special customers, we don't have to do this if you are going to be rude. After all the times I've been here you know I can't leave until you sign all the papers," the young dark-haired woman said as she held out a small clip board with the papers and a pen.

Ray looked at her and then realized that this was Rachel who had delivered to his house many times. "I'm sorry, Rachel. I just didn't know what to expect. I think Marcie left for good this morning with Ray Junior. I had this feeling like this was going to be the end, that you were somebody else and you were going to kill me."

"That's ridiculous. Why would you think that? Sometimes you have to ask yourself if everything you are thinking is just wrong," Rachel said.

Ray thought that Rachel had to be the biggest idiot that he'd ever heard speak. But, then Ray noticed a necklace around Rachel's neck and a pendant of a golden fish hung from the necklace rested on her collar bone. It was at that moment that there was a rare break in the clouds over Clatskanie, sunlight came through a break in the clouds and a ray of sunlight glinted off the golden fish pendant into Ray's eyes.

The light from the fish pendant transformed Ray, invaded his mind and his body like a disease, through his eyes, his nose, his mouth and his skin, sinking down into his head and into his stomach, soaking and infusing into his veins and his lungs, filling his clothes and supplanting him, overcoming Ray in every cell of his body. It was at this precise moment that Ray Cutter ceased to exist and I became the occupant of Ray Cutter's body. His body continued but it was inhabited by me. Ray Cutter was no more.

I took the clipboard from Rachel's hand. I felt the pressure building in my hands and I was overwhelmed by the feeling and the urge to write. I looked down at the paper on the clipboard which held nothing but blank medical forms. I took the pen and wrote "Facts are whores. You can dress them however you want. They do whatever you want," across the medical form.

Rachel could see what I wrote on the paper, especially the word "whore" and she did not say anything. She silently turned around, walked to her car and left without collecting her papers or clipboard. She never delivered to the house again.

I left the front door of my house open, it didn't matter anymore whether the doors, windows and curtains were closed up tight. I took the clipboard and the paper and my hands continued to write furiously across the blank medical forms, first filling one page with handwriting, then another page, then another, and so on. I wrote the rest of that day and all night stopping only to shake the cramps out of my hands. I continued to write with an out of control compulsion for the next 8 years.

Reader: This narrative is about my life and the transformation from Ray Cutter to me, your author. But, certain events in this narrative occurred in the life of Philip K. Dick and I am uncertain if they also occurred to Ray Cutter or me. Dick never lived in Oregon, as far as I know. Details like the Ovaltine, "I write with my hands", a deceased twin, the waiting headstone, 5 wives, the break-in, and the fish pendant, are all episodes in the life of Dick. Pure Dick details. Ray Cutter's life, my life and Dick's life have fused and are presented as an intertwined narrative which I cannot untangle. Some Dicksters may say I am taking Dick's identity or diluting his life by merging it with my own chronology, I'll let you decide.

AUTHORS

Gay Baines

Gay Baines lives in East Aurora, New York, and is a member of the *Roycroft Wordsmiths*. She has been writing since age eight. Her poetry has appeared in *Poet Lore*, *Rattapallax*, *Cimarron Review*, *Slipstream*, and other journals. She is co-founder and poetry editor of *July Literary Press* in Buffalo. In 2002 she published her first novel, "Dear M.K." A book of her selected poems, "Don't Let Go," was published in 2010. She is working desultorily on a chapbook, "The Book of Lies," and a short story collection, "Ancestor Worship," is under construction.

Debra Brenegan

Debra Brenegan has a Ph.D. in creative writing from The University of Wisconsin-Milwaukee and is an English Professor at Westminster College in Fulton, Missouri. For her fiction, she has received a Ragdale residency, and was a recent finalist for the *Snake Nation Press's* Serena McDonald Kennedy Award for a short-story collection, the John Gardner Memorial Fiction Prize, *The Cincinnati Review*'s Schiff Prose Prize, and the *Crab Creek Review* Fiction Prize. Her work has been published in journals such as *Calyx, Tampa Review, Natural Bridge, The Laurel Review, Cimarron Review, Milwaukee Magazine*, *Phoebe, RE:AL*, *The Southern Women's Review, Knee-Jerk, Literary Orphans, Circa Review,* and elsewhere. Her novel, "Shame the Devil" (*SUNY Press*), about nineteenth-century American journalist and novelist Fanny Fern, was named a finalist for *Foreword Reviews* 2011 Book of the Year Award for Historical Fiction.

Mark Burr

Mark Burr is a poet residing in historic Columbus, MS. He studied under the poet Kendall Dunkelberg. He likes squirrels, J.D. Salinger, Sylvia Plath, and movies about weird people. He is originally from Ocean Springs, MS.

Phil A. Carriere

"I received my MFA from the University of South Carolina in 2007. I am married to a beautiful woman 35 years and have two good and grown sons. I have been publishing poems in the small press magazines and journals since 1996. My work has appeared in *Blind*

Man's Rainbow, *Mid-West Poetry Review*, *Visions International* and others. For the last six years I have taught composition at a two year college in Columbia SC."

Rijn Collins

Rijn Collins is an Australian writer with a fondness for red notebooks, black coffee, and stories about circus folk. Her work has been published in numerous anthologies and literary journals, presented at the *Melbourne Emerging Writers Festival*, and adapted for performance on Australian and American radio. She's currently working on a novel, and trying not to include Elvis in it: so far, so good.

Jacob Collins-Wilson

Jacob Collins-Wilson, a high school English teacher, has had poetry published in *Barely South Review*, *Empirical Magazine*, *The Finger Literary Magazine*, *Pathos Literary Magazine* and *Burningword Literary Journal*, as well as a short essay published by *1 Bookshelf*. He can be reached by everyone at emailingjacob@gmail.com.

Darren C. Demaree

Darren C. Demaree is living in Columbus, Ohio with his wife and children. He is the author of "As We Refer to Our Bodies" (2013) and "Not for Art Nor Prayer" (2014), both are forthcoming from *8th House Publishing House*. He is the recipient of two Pushcart Prize nominations.

Jaimie Eubanks

Jaimie Eubanks lives, works and writes in Minneapolis. Her work can be found in places such as *Bartleby Snopes, Thought Catalog, Gloom Cupboard, The Journal of Truth and Consequence,* and *Monkey Bicycle.*

Matthew Fogarty

Born and raised in the square-mile suburbs of Detroit, Matthew Fogarty currently lives and writes in Columbia, where he is an MFA candidate at the University of South Carolina and fiction editor of *Yemassee*. He is the founder and co-editor of *Cartagena*, a literary journal. Matthew is analum of the Squaw Valley Community of Writers and the Wesleyan Writers Conference. His fiction has appeared or is forthcoming in such journals as *Midwestern Gothic, Revolution House, Umbrella Factory,* and *Zero Ducats.*

Allison Grayhurst

Allison Grayhurst has published in more than 160 international journals, magazines, and anthologies. Her book "Somewhere Falling" was published by *Beach Holme Publishers*, in Vancouver in 1995. Since then she has published ten other books of poetry and two collections with *Edge Unlimited Publishing*. Prior to the publication of "Somewhere Falling" she had a poetry book published, "Common Dream," and four chapbooks published by *The Plowman*. Her poetry chapbook "The River is Blind" was recently published by Ottawa publisher *above/ground press* December 2012. She lives in Toronto with her husband, two children, two cats, and a dog. She also sculpts, working with clay.

Kate Healey

Kate Healey is a gin enthusiast with an affinity for divination and walking by the sea with her loyal hound.

Holly Hendin

Holly Hendin is a psychiatrist working in Phoenix. In her poetry she tries to catch and elaborate on those moments that otherwise would slip by quietly. She hopes she is able to expand upon the spaces between the stitches of social relationships. Her poetry can be found in *ginosko, The Front Range Review, Summerset Review, The GW Review,* and *Schuylkill Valley Journal.*

J.B. Hogan

J. B. Hogan has over 240 stories and poems in such journals as: *Cynic Online Magazine, Istanbul Literary Review*, *Bewildering Stories*, *Every Day Poets*, *Ranfurly Review*, and the *Dead Mule.* His book "The Apostate" (fiction) is available from *Pen-L Publishing.* He lives in Fayetteville, Arkansas where, in addition to writing novels, stories and poems, he is involved in local history research, writing and teaching.

Gary F. Iorio

Gary F. Iorio was raised in Brooklyn and Massapequa New York. He currently works as a real estate attorney. His fiction, memoirs and poetry have appeared in numerous journals and newspapers, including *The East Hampton Star* and several past issues of *Crack the Spine.*

Peycho Kanev

Peycho Kanev is the author of 4 poetry collections and two chapbooks. He has won several European awards for his poetry and he's nominated for the Pushcart Award and Best of the Net. Translations of his books will be published soon in Italy, Poland and Russia. His poems have appeared in more than 900 literary magazines, such as: *Poetry Quarterly, Evergreen Review, Columbia College Literary Review, Hawaii Review, Cordite Poetry Review, Sheepshead Review, Off the Coast, The Adirondack Review, The Coachella Review, Two Thirds North, Sierra Nevada Review, The Cleveland Review* and many others.

Philip Kobylarz

Philip Kobylarz lives in the East Bay of San Francisco. Recent work of his appears or will appear in *Tampa Review, Apt, Santa Fe Literary Review, New American Writing, Prairie Schooner, Poetry Salzburg Review* and has appeared in *Best American Poetry*. His book, "rues," has recently been published by *Blue Light Press* of San Francisco.

Nick Kolakowski

Nick Kolakowski's work has appeared in *The Washington Post*, *McSweeney's*, *The Evergreen Review*, *Carrier Pigeon*, and other publications. His first book, a work of comedic nonfiction titled "How to Become an Intellectual," was published by *Adams Media* in 2012.

Darren R. Leo

Darren Leo holds an MFA in Fiction from Southern New Hampshire University. His work has appeared in several publications, and he is currently seeking representation for his novel. He resides in Rhode Island and is always seeking the right words.

Ashley Luster

Ashley Luster teaches first-year composition at Lewis and Clark Community College in Godfrey, IL. She resides in the nearby hipster town, Edwardsville, where she shares a tiny apartment with a tiny dog and an indecisive, slightly nutty, talented artist boyfriend named Jess.

Jason Lee Miller

Jason Lee Miller, MFA, is a curriculum developer and composition instructor at Eastern Kentucky University. His work --poetry, fiction, essays, and book reviews--have appeared or will appear in *94 Creations,*

Blood Lotus, the Bluegrass Accolade, the Copperfield Review, Danse Macabre Du Jour, Dew on the Kudzu, Eunoia, Gloom Cupboard, The Legendary, Milk Sugar, Numinous, Ontologica, Scarlet, State of Imagination, and *Subliminal Interiors.*

Amanda Mincher

Amanda Mincher is a writer and St. Louis native who holds an MFA in Fiction Writing from the University of Missouri - St. Louis. She has taught English and Composition at St. Louis Community College and Lindenwood University as well as worked as Associate Editor for *WomenArts Quartely* journal. She currently works in book production with *Elsevier*. Her work can be seen in *Bad Shoe Magazine*.

Alyssa Moore

Alyssa Moore is an undergraduate student currently pursuing her passion of creative writing at Susquehanna University in Pennsylvania.

Wendy Nardi

Wendy Nardi's fiction, poetry, essays and journalism have appeared in *Eclectica*, *360 Degrees: Art and LIterary Review*, *Skyline*, *Dance* and *High Performance* magazines, *The Boston Globe* and other publications. She was a staff writer for the *Kerouac Romnibus*, published by Penguin USA, and has received a Connecticut Artist Fellowship in Fiction Writing.

Aleksander Plonski

Aleksander Plonski was born in Poland in 1977 where he grew up, benefitting from the excellent education provided by the communist regime. By 1992, when he emigrated to the USA, he was already inspired by many of the British and American writers such as Blake, Whitman and Kerouac among many others. Since his arrival in Brooklyn, he has dedicated himself to the mastery of the written English language which culminated, in a way, when he graduated with honors in Philosophy and Literature in 2000. An author of innumerable poems and short stories he never pursued publication as much as the adventure of life. His story continues in Buenos Aires where he currently resides mending his broken heart and raising his 9 year old son. If you were to ask him, he would say that he was much more proud of surviving all the fucked up things he's done than of anything he had written - but then again, it's only the beginning.

Kris Price
Kris Price has an A.A. in Behavioral and Social Sciences from Modesto Junior College. He is currently attending University of Montana, Missoula where he is studying Creative Writing and Film Studies. Kris was an assistant editor for *Quercus Review*, and *Snail Mail Review*. He is working on his first chap book. His work has appeared in *Penumbra, Emerge, The Fine Line, the NewerYork Press, Diversion Press, Pressboard Press,* and the Modesto Poetry Anthology, *More than Soil, More than Sky.* He was awarded second place in Kay Ryan's Community College Poetry Project contest that she held during her term as the United States Poet Laureate.

Keith Rebec
Keith Rebec resides in the Upper Peninsula of Michigan. He's a graduate student working on an MA in Writing at Northern Michigan University. His writing has appeared in *Monkeybicycle*, *Underground Voices*, and *Split Lip Magazine*, among others.

Maggie Rehr
Every story Maggie writes is a culmination of all her temporary or current interests. Ghosts, incense, Robert Smith, or girls with too much cake. She aspires to bend the world, never break it, maybe just over-season it a bit. She hates apples, 80's beach music, and skeletons. She loves macaroni, steam, and Bob Dylan. She loves when you love the things she writes. Maggie has had her work published in Gone Lawn Web journal. She is nineteen and resides in Southeastern Pennsylvania.

Brian Rodan
Brian Rodan lives on the wet, west side of the Cascade Mountains in Washington State. From his window he overlooks a steep regrade which slouches down toward Puget Sound.

Eunice Tiptree
Eunice Tiptree has had poetry, fiction, and nonfiction published as both a man and a woman. Before transitioning to female in 2010-11, she was a journalist, writing on the space program for a dozen years. She has two degrees in journalism from Ohio University and a Masters in creative writing with distinction from Lancaster University,

England. She lives in Ohio with a black cat for good luck and is currently completing a memoir of her transition.

Abigail Warren

Abigail Warren lives in Northampton, Massachusetts and teaches at Cambridge College. Her work has appeared, or is forthcoming, in print and on-line, in *Monarch Review*, *Duct*, *Forge*, *Pearl, Brink Magazine*, *Gemini Magazine*, *Into The Teeth of the Wind*, *Sanskrit, Emerson Review, Hawai'i Pacific Review, The Clarion, Bluestem,* and *Compass Rose.* She was a recipient of the *Rosemary Thomas Poetry Prize.*

D.S. West

D.S. West is an experimental writer and artist currently emanating from Colorado. West's writing has appeared in *Elephant Journal*, *The New River Voice*, *From the Depths Online*, and the *Deep Cuts: Mayhem, Menace, and Misery* horror anthology.

Charles Wilkinson

Charles Wilkinson's publications include *The Pain Tree and Other Stories* (London Magazine Editions, 2000). His stories have appeared in *Best Short Stories 1990* (Heinemann), *Best English Short Stories 2* (Norton), *Midwinter Mysteries* (Little, Brown), *Unthology* (Unthank Books), *London Magazine* and in genre magazines such as *Supernatural Tales* and *Theaker's Quarterly Fiction.* "Ag & Au," a pamphlet of his poems, has just come out from *Flarestack Poets.*

Visit www.crackthespine.com to subscribe to our weekly digital magazine or to review our submission guidelines.

www.ingramcontent.com/pod-product-compliance
Lightning Source LLC
LaVergne TN
LVHW020715110826
845149LV00012B/2270

* 9 7 8 0 9 8 8 9 7 8 2 3 2 *